LUCY DANIELS

Animal Ark™

Puppy Puzzle
Kitten Crowd
Rabbit Race

LUCY DANIELS

Animal Ark™

Puppy
Puzzle

Illustrated by Paul Howard

Hodder
Children's
Books

A division of Hachette Children's Books

This edition of Puppy Puzzle, Kitten Crowd and Rabbit Race
first published in 1997

This edition published in 2008

ISBN-13: 978 0 340 95683 0

Puppy Puzzle

Special thanks to Helen Magee
Thanks also to C. J. Hall, B. Vet. Med., M.R.C.V.S. for reviewing
the veterinary information contained in this book.

Animal Ark Pets is a registered trademark of Working Partners Ltd.
Text copyright © 1996 Working Partners Ltd.
Created by Working Partners Limited, London W6 0QT
Original series created by Ben M. Baglio
Illustrations copyright © 1996 Paul Howard
Cover illustration by Chris Chapman

First published as a single volume in Great Britain in 1996
by Hodder Children's Books

The right of Lucy Daniels to be identified as the Author of
the Work has been asserted by her in accordance with the
Copyright, Designs and Patents Act 1988.

For more information about Animal Ark,
please contact www.animalark.co.uk

6

A Catalogue record for this book is available from the British Library

Typeset in Bembo by Avon DataSet Ltd,
Bidford-on-Avon, Warwickshire

Printed and bound in Great Britain by Clays Ltd, St Ives plc

The paper and board used in this paperback by Hodder Children's
Books are natural recyclable products made from wood grown in
sustainable forests. The manufacturing processes conform to the
environmental regulations of the country of origin.

Hodder Children's Books
a division of Hachette Children's Books
338 Euston Road, London NW1 3BH
An Hachette UK company
www.hachette.co.uk

Contents

1

Important news

Mandy Hope raced down the path to Animal Ark, hair flying. Would there be news today? She had been thinking about Molly all through school.

Molly was a black Labrador who was expecting puppies. Mrs Todd, Mandy's teacher, had smiled when Mandy told her why she was so excited.

"You and your animals, Mandy," she said. "Sometimes I think that's all you think about!"

Mandy grinned. She liked her teacher. Mrs Todd had a spaniel called Jodie. Mrs Todd liked animals too.

Mandy pushed open the front door of the cottage and raced through the hall to the back of the house, dropping her schoolbag as she ran.

She dashed into Animal Ark. Both of Mandy's parents were vets and their surgery was attached to the house.

"Hey! What's the hurry?" Jean Knox, the receptionist, called.

"Is there any news?" Mandy said in a rush. "Has Molly had her puppies?"

Jean smiled. "Your mum is just back from Moorcroft," she said. "Why don't you go and ask her all about it?"

Mandy bit her lip. "I won't be disturbing her, will I?" she said. "She hasn't got a patient with her?"

Jean shook her head. "No," she said. "Surgery is finished for the day. She's just

2

got to give the animals their medicines. You go ahead. Maybe she'll let you give her a hand. She's in the unit."

The unit was where animals could stay if they were too sick to go home.

Mandy shook her head. "I'm not allowed to help with the animals yet," she said. "But Dad says I can start helping out when I'm twelve." She sighed. "Twelve! Three whole years to go!"

Jean grinned. "I thought you were all excited about Molly and her puppies," she reminded her.

"I am," said Mandy. She rushed over to the door of the unit and pushed it open. "Hi, Mum," she said.

Mrs Hope was in the middle of examining a tortoise. But the tortoise didn't seem to want to come out of its shell. "Mandy!" she said. "Guess what?"

"Molly's puppies have arrived!" said Mandy.

Mrs Hope laughed. "Five of them," she said. "And all healthy."

Mandy sighed with relief. She knew

her mother had been worried about Molly. Mrs Lawson at Moorcroft Farm bred Labradors and Molly was one of her best mums. But Molly was getting a bit old for motherhood now and Mrs Lawson had decided that this was to be her last litter.

"And Molly is OK?" said Mandy.

Mrs Hope nodded. "She's fine," she said. "And as proud as Punch. You'd think she'd never had puppies before."

"When can I see them?" Mandy asked.

"Give Molly a few days," said Mrs Hope. "Let her settle in with her puppies. Then I'll take you up to see them."

"Terrific!" Mandy said.

Moorcroft Farm was about two miles outside Welford, the village where Mandy lived. The farm was high up on the Yorkshire moors and Mandy loved going there. Mandy loved going *anywhere* so long as there were animals to visit.

Mrs Hope turned back to the tortoise just as he popped his head out of his shell.

"Toto is looking a lot better," she said.

"Did you give Jill that leaflet on caring for tortoises?"

Mandy nodded. "Jill was really pleased with it," she said. "She promised to learn it by heart."

Jill Redfern was in Mandy's class at school. Toto was her tortoise, and had nearly died because Jill had let him hibernate too long.

Mandy put her finger very gently on Toto's head. "Hello, Toto," she said. "How are you feeling today? You're

5

going to see Jill later. She's coming to visit you."

"*Who's* coming over?" said a voice from the door.

Mandy turned as her father came into the unit and dumped his bag on the counter. He had dark hair and a beard and the kind of smile that made you want to smile too.

"Jill Redfern," Mandy said. Then she remembered the really important news. "Oh, Dad," she said, "Molly's had her puppies!"

Mr Hope looked across at his wife. "All well?" he said.

Mrs Hope nodded. "Perfect," she replied. "One of the puppies is a bit on the small side, though. He'll need a little extra care."

"But he will be all right, won't he?" Mandy asked anxiously.

Emily Hope gave Toto a pat and put him back in his cage. "Of course he will," she said. "He just needs someone to love him and take care of him. Mrs

Lawson will find him a good owner."

"What about me?" Mandy said hopefully. "*I* could look after him."

Mr and Mrs Hope looked at each other.

"You know the rules, Mandy," Mr Hope said.

Mandy sighed. She loved her parents being vets, it meant there were always animals around. But they were so busy with everyone else's pets, they didn't have time for any of their own.

"What's for tea?'" said Mr Hope, changing the subject. "I'm starving."

Mrs Hope laughed. "You're going to have to take up jogging if you don't watch out," she said.

Mr Hope's eyes twinkled. "*After* tea," he said.

Mrs Hope moved towards the door. "Come along, Mandy," she said. "Aren't you hungry?"

"Starving!" said Mandy. "But just let me say goodbye to Toto."

Mrs Hope smiled. "Of course," she said.

Mandy turned to the tortoise.

"I'll miss you when you go home," she said softly to the little animal. "But you're going to be well looked after from now on, Toto."

Mrs Hope stood by the door waiting for her.

"You really do love animals, don't you, Mandy?" she said.

Mandy nodded and smiled up at her mother. "Of course I do," she said. "More than anything. And I want to be just like you and Dad when I grow up. I want to be a vet too."

Her mum smiled. "Let's wait and see," she said. "It'll be a long time before you're grown up. You might change your mind!"

Mandy didn't say anything. But she knew she wouldn't ever change her mind. There was nothing in the world as important to her as animals.

2

Puppy wanted

Next day Mandy was so eager to tell everybody about Molly's puppies that she raced across the playground without looking where she was going. As she turned the corner of the school building she banged straight into someone coming from the opposite direction.

"Ouch!" said Mandy, rubbing her nose.

"Ow!" said a voice and Mandy looked down.

A boy was sitting on the ground, rubbing his head. A pair of spectacles hung from one ear.

"Sorry," said Mandy. "I shouldn't have been running."

The boy looked up and put his glasses back on. "Neither should I," he said. "Is your nose all right?"

Mandy gave it another rub. "I don't think it's broken," she said.

The boy grinned. "You're Mandy Hope, aren't you?" he said. "From Animal Ark."

Mandy looked at him. "I know you," she said. "You've got a cat called Benji." She frowned. "The only thing is I can't remember *your* name."

"James Hunter," said the boy, standing up. "I'm in the class below you – Mrs Black's class."

Mandy was thinking. "Benji had an eye infection last month, didn't he?" she said.

James nodded. "Your dad gave him some drops and he's fine now."

Mandy smiled. "I'm glad," she said.

James had his glasses on properly now. If he was in the class below her, he must be about eight years old. He had brown hair that flopped over his eyes and his glasses were already beginning to slide down his nose. He pushed them back up again.

"So why were you in such a rush?" asked Mandy.

James flushed and shook his hair out of his eyes. "I was in a hurry to get to the news bulletin board," he said. "I've got something to pin up."

"What?" asked Mandy.

"A sort of advert," James said.

The news bulletin board was terrific. It was only a big pin board on the wall of the main school hall but you could put all sorts of messages on it. So, if you wanted to sell your bike, or if you'd got your swimming proficiency certificate, you could let everybody know.

The main hall was going to have some building work done to it this term. Mandy hoped they wouldn't lose the bulletin board. It was a great way of finding out what was going on in Welford.

"That's where *I* was going," said Mandy. "I've got some news as well."

Just then the bell rang and Mandy and James looked at each other.

"Come on," said Mandy. "We'll just have time to pin our notices up if we hurry!"

They raced round to the front door of the school and into the main hall. As usual there was a crowd round the bulletin board. Mandy and James had to squeeze past several people to get near it.

"Come on, Mandy," Jill said as she hurried past. "You'll be late."

"I won't be a moment," Mandy said.

Jill looked back over her shoulder. "How was Toto this morning?" she asked.

"Mum says you can take him home tomorrow," Mandy said. "She was really impressed when I told her how much you knew about tortoises."

Jill yelled "Yippee!" and raced off down the corridor.

Mandy grinned. Jill must have done an awful lot of work. She had been word perfect when she came round to Animal Ark last night. Mandy reckoned she must be able to recite that tortoise information leaflet in her sleep now.

Mandy unzipped her schoolbag and pulled out the notice she had written. She pinned it up on the board and stood back, looking at it.

CONGRATULATIONS TO MOLLY,
THE BEST LABRADOR
IN THE WORLD.
FIVE PUPPIES!
ALL DOING WELL.

The bell stopped ringing and James pulled a face. "I'll get in trouble with Mrs Black if I'm late again," he said. He pushed a pin into the bulletin board and looked at his notice. "There," he said. "Got to go. Bye, Mandy!"

"Bye!" said Mandy.

Then James was off, racing down the corridor. He looked back. "Nice running into you," he joked.

But Mandy wasn't listening. She was looking at the notice James had pinned up.

<u>WANTED</u>
PUPPY
GOOD HOME
CONTACT JAMES HUNTER

Mandy stared at the notice for a moment. Then she turned and looked for James. He was already halfway along the corridor, heading for his classroom.

"James!" she called.

He looked round.

"Meet me here at break," she shouted.

James looked puzzled.

"Why?" he called back.

"I've just had the most terrific idea!" said Mandy.

3

The best of friends

Mandy could hardly wait for break. She rushed out into the playground as soon as the bell rang.

"Hi, James!" she yelled as James came across from the other side of the playground.

"Well?" he said, coming over. "What's your wonderful idea? I'm dying to know!"

"It's about your puppy," Mandy said.

James looked puzzled. "I haven't got a puppy," he said. "That was what my notice was about. I *want* a puppy. Mum and Dad have promised to buy me one. But I don't have one yet."

"I know," said Mandy. "But you didn't see the notice *I* put up, did you?"

James shook his head. "No – what was it about?" he said.

"You know Mrs Lawson at Moorcroft Farm?" Mandy asked.

James thought for a moment. "Oh, yes," he said. "She breeds dogs, doesn't she?"

Mandy nodded. "She breeds Labradors. And Molly, one of her Labradors, has just had a litter of puppies."

She looked at James, her eyes sparkling. "Mrs Lawson will be looking for good homes for them. How would you like an adorable Labrador puppy, James?"

James looked at her for a moment, then he grinned. "Oh, I would," he said. "A Labrador! Do you think she would really let me have one?"

Mandy smiled. "I'm sure she would," she said. "I'm going up to Moorcroft with Mum to see the puppies soon. Why don't you come along and have a look at them?"

James's eyes lit up. "Could I?" he said.

Mandy nodded. "You could see if you like any of them," she said.

"And you could help me choose," James said. "You know such a lot about animals, Mandy."

Mandy shook her head. "Not *such* a

19

lot," she said. "But I'm learning. I've got all sorts of books about animals. And I'd love to help you choose a puppy."

"Maybe I could borrow a book about Labradors," James said shyly.

Mandy smiled. "Of course you can," she said. "Come over to Animal Ark after school and I'll lend you one."

By the time the bell rang for the end of break, Mandy and James had made a plan.

"Mum!" Mandy called, rushing into Animal Ark after school.

"In here," her mother called back.

Mandy dumped her schoolbag and raced into the kitchen. She loved the kitchen at Animal Ark. It had oak beams and bright red curtains at the windows. And there was a huge pine table in the middle of the room. Mrs Hope was sitting at it with Mandy's grandmother.

"Oh, hi, Gran," Mandy said, her eyes lighting up. She looked at the plate of fluffy yellow scones on the table. "Did you make those?"

Gran's eyes twinkled. "I certainly did," she said. "They're newly baked this afternoon. Come and have one."

"Not before you've washed your hands," said Mrs Hope.

Mandy went to the sink. "Oh, Mum, you'll never guess," she said. "James Hunter's parents want to buy him a puppy and I told him about Molly. Can he come with us to see the pups and choose one? I said he could and he's coming round in a little while to see what you think. *And* I've promised to lend him a book on Labradors. Don't you think it would be *wonderful* if he took one? Then we'd have one of Molly's puppies living right here in the village!"

"Heavens!" said Gran. 'You're like a runaway train."

Mrs Hope laughed. "Have a glass of milk, Mandy," she said. "And why don't you try all that again? What's this about James Hunter and a puppy?"

Mandy sat down at the table and poured herself some milk from the big blue and white striped jug. Gran put a plate with a buttered scone on it in front of her.

"Now," said Gran, "why don't you start at the beginning?"

Mandy took a deep breath and went through the story again.

"I think that's a splendid idea," Mrs Hope said when she had finished. "Tell James he's welcome to come to Moorcroft with us."

The door bell rang and Mandy jumped up. "I will," she said. "That'll be him now. He only popped home to tell his mum he was coming round here."

Gran and Mrs Hope looked at each other. "Just as well I made a double batch of scones then, isn't it?" Gran said as Mandy ran to let James in.

James came into the kitchen, looking earnestly at Mrs Hope.

"Mandy has told us all about you getting a puppy, James," Mrs Hope said.

"Now, sit down and have some scones and a glass of milk and tell me when you'd like to go to Moorcroft."

"Oh, as soon as possible!" James said eagerly. He sat down beside Mandy at the table.

Gran laughed. "Just like Mandy," she said. "Always in a hurry."

James flushed. "Oh, sorry," he said. "I mean, whenever you think."

Mrs Hope looked at him. "But the sooner the better?" she said gently.

James smiled up at her. "Oh, yes," he said. "You don't know how much I want a puppy of my own. My parents want one too. The sooner the better!"

Gran looked at Mandy and James sitting side by side at the table. "Something tells me you two are going to become the best of friends," she said.

"We already are," Mandy said. "James loves animals. So of *course* we're the best of friends!"

4

A puppy for James

Next day at assembly Mandy sat down beside Sarah Drummond. Sarah was in her class. James was sitting behind them. He leaned over and spoke to Mandy.

"I've been reading that book you gave me," he said. "It's going to be brilliant having a puppy! I think Labradors must be the smartest dogs in the world."

"Are you getting a puppy?" said Sarah. "So am I."

Mandy turned to her. "I didn't know you liked dogs," she said.

Sarah put her nose in the air. "This isn't just *any* puppy," she said. "It's a pedigree."

Mandy bit her lip. "*All* puppies are lovely," she said. "It doesn't matter whether they're cross-breeds or pedigrees. They're all animals."

"Shh!" said James. "Listen!"

Mandy looked up. Mrs Garvie, the Headteacher, was standing on the platform at the front of the hall.

"Before you go to class," she said, "I have an announcement to make. We've decided that the last day of the summer term will be Pet Day."

There was a murmur of voices as the pupils turned to one another excitedly.

Mrs Garvie held up her hand for silence. "All of you will be able to bring your pets to school on that day." She smiled. "Just so long as we don't have any *dangerous* animals."

"Like tigers," said Peter Foster from the row in front of Mandy.

"No tigers, please, Peter. Timmy will be quite enough of a handful!" Mrs Garvie said and everybody laughed.

Peter went bright red.

Timmy was Peter's cairn terrier, and he was the naughtiest dog in the village.

"Oh, excellent!" said James. "I'll be able to bring my new puppy."

Sarah looked at him. "And I'll be able to bring *mine*," she said. "I bet mine will be nicer than yours." She looked at Mandy. "Do *you* have a pet?"

Mandy suddenly felt sad. "No," she said. "I don't have a pet of my own."

Sarah looked surprised. "Fancy that," she said. "Imagine living at Animal Ark and not having a pet! I feel quite sorry for you."

Mandy bit her lip. Sarah didn't *sound* sorry for her. But she didn't say anything to the other girl.

Mrs Garvie warned the children to keep out of the way of the builders who were coming to work on the school hall. Then she announced the end of assembly. Everyone got up to go.

"Sarah doesn't really feel sorry for me," Mandy said to James as they filed out of the hall.

James looked at Mandy. "Don't be upset about Sarah," he said. "She didn't mean it."

Mandy tried to smile but she still felt sad. "Sometimes I wish I had a pet of my own," she said.

James smiled. "You've got a whole ark full of pets!" he said. "Maybe your mum and dad would let you bring one of *them*?"

Mandy shook her head. "Oh, no," she said, "they wouldn't let me do that. All the animals at Animal Ark are patients."

"Oh, I see," said James.

Mandy smiled. "But *you'll* have a pet to bring," she said. "You'll have your very own puppy by the end of the summer term!"

★ ★ ★

"It's not far now," said Mrs Hope as the Land-rover swung round a bend on the road to Moorcroft Farm.

James was trying to look relaxed but Mandy could see that he was really excited and nervous.

Mrs Hope looked round. "I hope Benji won't feel put out when you bring a puppy home," she said.

James looked worried. "Do you think he'll be jealous?" he asked.

Mrs Hope shrugged. "Maybe you should keep him away from the puppy for a little while," she said. "Benji's bound to feel a bit protective about his own territory. After all, he's been the only pet in your house for a long time now. But they'll soon get used to each other."

"I hope so," said James. "I wouldn't like Benji to feel bad."

"He won't," said Mandy. "Just make sure you don't ignore him when the new puppy arrives."

"You might even have to make more

fuss of him than usual," said Mrs Hope.

"That's no problem," James said. "I like making a fuss of Benji."

The Land-rover turned into the farm track that led to Moorcroft.

"Oh, look," said Mandy, pointing to a car parked in the farmyard. "That isn't Mrs Lawson's car. I wonder whose it is."

"Maybe somebody else has come to look at the puppies," Mrs Hope said.

Mrs Hope drew the Land-rover to a halt and Mandy and James jumped out.

"Let's go and see," said Mandy. She raced across the farmyard towards the house.

"Wait for me!" James called, running after her.

"Mrs Lawson, we're here!" Mandy shouted, knocking on the back door.

Mrs Lawson came to meet them. She was a friendly-looking lady with grey hair and an old tweed skirt.

"So I see," she said, smiling. "Come on into the back kitchen. Molly's there with her pups. And don't make too much noise. She's already had one visitor today."

Mandy immediately clapped a hand to her mouth. "Sorry," she whispered. "Are the puppies asleep?"

Mrs Lawson grinned. "They're only a few days old," she said. "Puppies that age are usually asleep — when they aren't eating, that is."

Mandy and James tiptoed after her into the farmhouse's warm back kitchen.

"There you are," said Mrs Lawson.

Mandy and James looked where she was pointing. A big wicker basket was drawn up beside the bright red Aga and Molly was curled up in it. As she lifted her head towards them Mandy got her first glimpse of the puppies, snuggled up close to their mother.

"Oh, look, James!" she said, walking softly across the floor towards the basket. "Aren't they wonderful?"

James came and stood beside her, looking down at the puppies. Five tiny balls of black fur were curled up against their mother. One of them yawned and

Mandy could see his little pink tongue.
But he kept his eyes tightly closed.

"Their eyes won't open for another
week yet," said Mrs Lawson.

"Oh, look," said Mandy. "Look at that
tiny one, the one that just yawned. Isn't
he sweet!"

Mrs Lawson came to stand beside her.
"I was worried about him at first," she
said. "But he's a strong little fellow. He's
going to be all right."

"Is that the one Mum was talking

about?" said Mandy. "The littlest one of the litter?"

Mrs Lawson nodded. "He might be little but he's a real character," she said. "He's got a lovely friendly nature."

"Are we allowed to touch the puppies?" James asked.

Mrs Lawson smiled. "Of course," she said.

James bent down and gazed at the smallest puppy. He stretched out a finger and touched the puppy very gently. The little animal gave a tiny squeak.

"Did you hear that?" said James. "He said hello."

Mrs Lawson laughed. "He certainly did, James."

James turned a shining face to Mandy. "I know which one I want," he said.

"Just so long as it's not the one I've chosen!" said a voice from the door.

Mandy and James turned round. Sarah Drummond was standing there.

"Mummy wants to have a word with you, Mrs Lawson," she said.

Mrs Lawson nodded and walked towards the door.

"Are you adopting one of Molly's puppies too?" Mandy asked Sarah.

Sarah nodded. "I'm having the biggest one," she said. "He's beautiful."

James smiled. "That's all right then," he said. "The one I want is the smallest of them all."

Mrs Lawson looked back at him from the doorway. "Are you sure?" she said. "He'll be a bit more work than a big one. You'll need to feed him more often, for starters."

"How often?" asked Mandy.

"Five times a day to begin with," said Mrs Lawson. "Puppies need lots of milk and high protein food to help them grow."

James looked worried. "How will I know what kind of food to give him?" he said.

"I'll give you a diet sheet," said Mrs Lawson. "Puppies aren't so very different from human babies. They need just as much care and attention. You start them off on milk and then go on to a little porridge or cereal. And after that you can introduce some fish and meat scraps. But they *are* a lot of work. Are you sure you can cope?"

James pushed his glasses up his nose and nodded. "I'm sure," he said. "And this is the puppy I want. I couldn't have any other. He's perfect."

"And I'll help James to look after him," said Mandy.

Mrs Lawson smiled. "Well, good for you, James," she said. "I think you've made a very good choice there." And she went out of the room.

Sarah looked down into the basket. "*That* little thing!" she said. "Wait till Pet Day. I bet my puppy is twice as big as yours by then!"

Mandy turned to her and smiled. "They'll both be lovely," she said.

But Sarah shook her head. "Mine will be much nicer," she said. "And *you* won't even have a pet to bring to Pet Day."

Mandy's face fell and James stepped forward.

"Oh yes she will," he said.

Sarah and Mandy looked at him in surprise.

"You know I won't," Mandy said.

"What pet?" said Sarah.

James looked down at the puppy he had chosen.

"My puppy," he said. "Mandy is going to help me look after him. We'll share him. We'll both bring him to Pet Day."

Sarah looked put out but Mandy smiled and gave James a grateful look.

"Oh, James," she said. "Are you sure? Can I really share the puppy with you?"

"Of course you can," James said. "How am I going to learn to look after him without your help?"

Mandy looked down at Molly. "There, Molly," she said. "I'm going to be looking after one of your puppies. Isn't that wonderful?"

"Sharing a pet!" said Sarah. "Who ever heard of that?" And she flounced off out of the door.

5

A new home

It was six weeks before Mrs Lawson would let the puppies leave their mother. But she told Mandy and James they could come and see the puppy as often as they liked. Mr Hunter took Mandy and James to see him every week.

The puppy opened his eyes when he was ten days old and by the end of the second week he was beginning to cut his first teeth. James could hardly wait to get him home.

"I know what I'm going to call him," he said at the end of their second visit.

"What?" said Mandy.

"Blackie," James said.

Mandy looked down at the little black bundle of fur.

"That's perfect, James," she said.

Mr Hunter smiled. "That's a good name," he said. "You'll need to get him used to it as soon as possible."

"That's true," Mrs Lawson said. "It's never too early to get a puppy used to his name. Try it out on him now, James."

James bent down and tickled his puppy under the chin. The little dog yawned and looked up at him sleepily.

"Hello, Blackie," James said. "How do you like your name?"

Blackie yawned again and snuggled closer to his mother. His eyes closed.

"He's gone back to sleep again!" said Mandy.

"Maybe you should call him Sleepy," Mr Hunter joked.

James shook his head. "I've made up my mind," he said. "He's Blackie!"

When it was time for Blackie to leave his mother Mr Hope took Mandy and James up to collect him. Mr Hope was going to check on all the puppies before they went off to their new owners.

Mrs Lawson had put the puppies in a playpen. They rolled around, chasing one another and having pretend fights. Mr Hope looked at the little animals tumbling around.

"Which one is yours, James?" he said.

James pointed Blackie out and Mr Hope watched the puppy for a moment.

"He looks a good one," he said. "Look how he's playing with the others. He's got plenty of confidence but he isn't aggressive. He's a fine, lively puppy."

"Have you got owners for all of them, Mrs Lawson?" Mandy said.

Mrs Lawson nodded. "All the ones I'm

selling," she said. "There was no trouble finding good homes for them. Let me get yours for you, James."

She bent down to pick up a puppy.

"Not that one, Mrs Lawson," Mandy called out. "That isn't James's."

James came to look. "No," he said. "There's mine. The little one."

"My, my," Mrs Lawson said. "You're right of course. This one is Sarah's. How silly of me."

She picked up James's puppy and looked at him. "These two are very alike," she said.

"James's puppy really has grown a lot," said Mandy.

"But he's still a *little* smaller," said James.

"I would know your puppy anywhere, James," Mandy said. "Blackie's got such a nice look in his eyes. He's so friendly."

Mrs Lawson laughed. "You're very observant, Mandy," she said. "I'm glad I didn't get these two mixed up!"

James held out his arms and Mrs Lawson gave him the puppy. The little

animal squeaked and looked up at his new owner. His tiny pink tongue came out and he licked James's hand.

James looked at Mandy. "I can't believe it," he said. "My very own puppy!"

Mandy put out a hand and stroked the puppy's soft coat.

"He's beautiful," she said softly. "The nicest of the lot!"

Mr Hope looked at Blackie. "You know, I think you're right, Mandy," he said. "Look how easily he lets James handle him. And see the way he's looking back at James. That's the mark of a confident animal."

James cradled Blackie in the crook of his arm. "He's so good-natured," he said.

Mr Hope nodded. "Turn him on his back, James," he said. "Let's see how he reacts."

James turned Blackie over. The puppy squirmed a little and then lay contentedly in James's arms.

"There, you see," said Mr Hope. "That's what you're looking for in a puppy. A bit of a struggle and then he settles down quickly. I'd say you've got a fine puppy there, James."

"Of course he has," Mandy said. "All Molly's puppies are wonderful, aren't they, girl?" She turned to look down at Molly.

The Labrador looked up at her with sad eyes.

"Oh, Molly," Mandy said. "You're going to miss your puppies, aren't you?" she said.

Mrs Lawson gave Molly a pat. "I'm keeping one of the puppies to breed from," she said. "So Molly won't lose all of her family."

Mandy smiled. It was good to think of Molly still having one of her puppies to look after.

Mr and Mrs Hunter were waiting eagerly for them to arrive home with the puppy.

"I've got his bed all ready," said Mrs Hunter. "Bring him straight into the kitchen."

Mandy followed James and Blackie into the kitchen. There were newspapers spread out over the kitchen floor.

"Just in case of accidents," Mrs Hunter said.

Mr Hope nodded. "Very wise," he said. "You can't always get a puppy of that age outside in time!"

Mandy looked at the dog basket in the corner of the room. There was a cardboard box inside it.

"What's that for?" she said.

"The dog basket is too big for him at the moment," Mr Hunter said. "But if we put him in a box inside the basket, then he'll get used to it."

"That's a good idea," said Mandy.

"And I've put an old blanket in the bottom of the box," said James. "So Blackie will be really cosy."

"If he misses his mother you could put a hot-water bottle in beside him," said Mr Hope. "But make sure it has a cover on it."

James nodded. "I'll do that," he said.

"Blackie is sure to miss Molly at first."

Blackie looked up at him and gave a soft little growl.

"Did you hear that?" said James. "I think he knows his name already."

"Maybe he's hungry," said Mandy. "Mrs Lawson said we should give him something to eat when we got him home."

Mr Hope looked at his watch. "I must get back to the surgery," he said. "Give him something to eat now, James. Some warm milk with a little cereal and grated vegetables should do. And don't forget to take him outside immediately afterwards. House-training can't begin too soon!"

"Can Mandy stay for tea?" James asked.

Mr Hope and the Hunters looked at one another.

"I don't think I could drag her away if I wanted to!" said Mr Hope, laughing.

Mrs Hunter looked at Mandy. She and James were already gathering things toge-ther for Blackie's feed.

"Something tells me you aren't going

to see too much of Mandy for a while,"
she said to Mr Hope.

6

An escape

Mandy went round to James's house every day after school. They had tried the hot-water bottle trick and Blackie was settling in well. In fact he was getting very adventurous, starting to explore his new home. Benji the cat was also interested in Blackie. But poor little Blackie was terrified of him. Not that Benji would hurt Blackie. He only wanted to play.

By the time Blackie was ten weeks old there were fewer puddles on the kitchen floor for Mandy and James to mop up and the puppy was eating some solid food. Toilet-training was pretty important so Mandy and James made a big effort.

"We have to find a way of telling him to perform," said James. "We should use the same words each time so that he'll know what to do."

"And we need to make sure we always take him to the same place in the garden," said Mandy.

"That's OK," James said. "Dad has fenced off a corner especially for him, so as long as we take him out straight after meals there shouldn't be any accidents. But we have to clean up after him."

"Of course we will," said Mandy. "It would be good to get him properly trained before we start taking him out for walks."

They would be allowed to take him

out in three or four weeks' time – once his injections had been completed. But for now, they had to keep him in the garden or carry him if they wanted to take him out of the house.

On Friday evening Mandy knocked on the Hunters' door as usual.

"James is in the kitchen," Mrs Hunter said to Mandy.

Mandy made her way to the kitchen and pushed open the door.

"Hi, Mandy!" James said, then looked behind her. "Shut the door," he said. "Quick!"

Mandy turned to close the door but she was too slow. Benji shot through her legs into the kitchen.

"Oh, no!" she said, making a dive for Benji. "Sorry, James. I forgot."

James darted towards the dog basket but he was too late. A bundle of black fur scrambled out of the cardboard box and over the side of the basket, skidding across the kitchen floor. Benji made a

dash for the puppy but the little animal scampered out of the kitchen and down the hall.

"Oh, no!" said James. "Where has he *gone*?"

Mandy groaned. "I left the door open. What an idiot I am!"

James made a dive for Benji and gathered him up in his arms. "It's OK," he said. He looked down at Benji. "We know you wouldn't hurt the puppy," he said. "But you do frighten him."

Mandy took Benji into the sitting-room and explained to Mrs Hunter what had happened.

"Don't you worry, Mandy," Mrs Hunter said. "I'll keep Benji here. You two search for Blackie."

Mandy found James in the hall.

"I think he's in there," said James pointing to the cupboard under the stairs. The door was slightly open.

"If your hall cupboard is anything like ours, it'll take ages to find him," said Mandy. "But nothing could be as bad as ours."

James pulled open the door. The cupboard was filled with golf clubs and tennis rackets, umbrellas and boxes and all *sorts* of things.

"I take that back," said Mandy. "It's even *worse* than ours!"

"Mum is always saying we need to clear it out," James said.

"Oh well, let's have a look with the light on," said Mandy.

James shook his head. "There isn't a

light," he said. "Dad is always meaning to put one in."

Mandy peered into the deep recesses of the cupboard. "How on earth are we going to find a black puppy in a pitch-black cupboard?" she said.

James pushed his glasses up on to his nose. "We'll just have to shift all this stuff until we find him," he said.

"Or tempt him out," said Mandy. "I'll go and get him something to eat."

"Good idea," said James, lifting a golf bag out of the cupboard. "Here, Blackie!" he called hopefully.

By the time Mandy got back with a bowl of milk James had dragged a pile of stuff out of the cupboard. But there was still no sign of the puppy.

Mandy put the bowl down on the floor. Then she and James crouched down and waited. There was a scuffling noise at the back of the cupboard, then the scratching of tiny nails. Very slowly a small black head peered out from behind a cardboard box.

Mandy held her breath. She didn't want to scare Blackie. The puppy nosed gently at the side of the cardboard box then crept round it, sniffing as he caught the scent of milk. Slowly, his eyes flicking from the milk to Mandy and James, he crept closer until he was beside the bowl.

Mandy and James stayed perfectly still until Blackie put his head down and began to lap. James let him polish off all the milk before he scooped him up into his arms and gave him a cuddle.

"Naughty Blackie!" he said.

Mandy grinned. "At least he got an extra feed," she said. "If that happens very often he'll soon put on weight."

James looked at the puppy proudly. "He *is* getting bigger, isn't he?" he said. "Soon he'll be as big as Sarah's puppy."

"Sooty," said Mandy.

"Is that what she's called him?" James asked. "Of course, he's as black as Blackie."

Mandy gave Blackie a pat. "I wonder if he gets into as much mischief as Blackie does," she said. Then she laughed. "He was completely invisible in that dark cupboard. You certainly picked the right name for him, James."

James tickled the puppy under the chin. "Oh, Blackie," he said. "What *will* you get up to next?"

7

"Sit!"

Mandy looked up from the book she was reading. It was called *You and Your Dog*.

She looked across the Hunters' kitchen table at James. James also had his nose buried deep in a book. Blackie was curled up fast asleep in his basket.

"You know, James," she said, "it's time to start thinking about Blackie's obedience training. After all, he's twelve weeks old now."

James looked up from his book. "I know," he said. "But how can we train him with Benji around? Blackie still runs away every time he sees Benji."

"We could take him to Animal Ark," Mandy said.

James shook his head. "Blackie hasn't had all his injections yet," he said. "We can't let him into contact with other animals in case he picks up an infection. There are too many animals coming in and out of the surgery. We need somewhere quiet with no other animals."

"And somewhere that Blackie can't get out of," said Mandy.

"He's good at getting out of places," James said. "He nearly got out of the garden yesterday."

The back door opened and Mrs Hunter came in just in time to hear James's last words. "I tore a new pair of tights scrabbling in the hedge to catch him," she said.

Blackie stirred and sat up, blinking at the sound of her voice.

"Now, don't you go getting into any more mischief," Mrs Hunter scolded him.

The front door bell rang. She put her shopping basket down on the floor and went out to answer the door.

Mandy was still thinking about Blackie's training. "We could take him to Gran and Grandad's," she said. "Grandad has just put a new fence all round their garden. Even Blackie couldn't get out of it."

James pushed his book aside, looking hopeful. Blackie scrambled out of his basket and scampered across the floor. "That's a great idea," James said. Then he looked at Blackie. "Oh, no!" he said. "Blackie, *no!*"

The little dog was tugging at a paper bag in Mrs Hunter's shopping basket. The bag burst open and several cream buns rolled across the floor. Blackie pounced on one of them and began licking up the cream.

The kitchen door opened before Mandy or James could get to Blackie.

"What on earth . . . ?" began Mrs Hunter, as she came back in. Then she looked at James. "It's high time that puppy started learning how to behave himself!" she said.

James looked at Mandy. "Are you sure your gran and grandad would let us train Blackie at their house?"

Mandy smiled. "Of course they would," she said. "They'd love it. Just you wait and see."

"Sit!" James said sternly.

It was Saturday and Mandy and James were in the back garden of Lilac Cottage, Mandy's grandparents' house.

Blackie looked up at James and wagged his tail.

"Maybe if you pushed his bottom down at the same time as you say 'sit'," suggested Mandy.

James looked at her in despair. "I've tried that," he said.

Mandy bit her lip. They'd been trying to train Blackie for two weeks now and were getting nowhere fast.

The little puppy looked eagerly at them, jumping up and resting his paws against James's jeans. Mandy moved a few metres away and looked at Blackie.

"Stay!" she said in a firm voice.

Blackie immediately scampered towards her.

"It's hopeless," said Mandy, laughing. "I don't think we'll ever train him!"

"Sooty always sits when I tell him to," said a voice behind them.

"Sarah!" said Mandy, turning round.

Sarah was standing at the back garden gate with Sooty in her arms.

"Does he really sit when you tell him to?" asked James, coming over. "Let's see. I don't know how you get him to do as he's told."

Sarah drew back, cradling Sooty in her arms. "I can't," she said. "Not here. He's still got one more lot of injections to go and I'm not allowed to put him down outside until he's had all of them."

Mandy nodded. "Blackie gets his final lot next week," she said. "We had to carry him all the way here. But he can run about in the garden. That's quite safe."

Sarah put her nose in the air. "Run about is right," she said. "Where has he gone?"

Mandy and James looked round.

"Blackie!" James called. "Blackie, where are you?"

"Huh!" said Sarah. "He doesn't even answer to his name. Just you wait and see what Sooty can do at the Pet Day." And she strode off down the lane.

Mandy and James looked at each other.

"Where is he?" said Mandy.

Grandad came round the side of the potting shed.

"Oh, Grandad, have you seen Blackie?" asked Mandy.

"I certainly have. He was in among my raspberry canes," Grandad said.

Mandy looked up at him. "Oh, no!" she said.

Grandad's eyes twinkled. "It's all right," he said. "I caught him before he did much harm."

"But where is he now?" said James.

Grandad rubbed his nose. "Mandy's gran has him in the house," he said. "She's taken a real fancy to the little fellow."

Mandy smiled. "I knew it was a good idea to bring him to Lilac Cottage," she said.

"So how is the training going?" Grandad asked.

Mandy and James looked at one another.

"It isn't very easy," James said.

"Blackie looks at us with those big brown eyes of his," Mandy said.

"And you can't bear to scold him?" Grandad said.

Mandy nodded. "He's such a darling," she said.

Grandad grunted. "If he gets in among my raspberry canes again he won't be a darling to me," he said.

Mandy bit her lip. She knew Grandad didn't mean it. He was just as fond of Blackie as Gran was. But she and James didn't seem to be making much progress with Blackie's training. Maybe they weren't being firm enough with him.

The back door opened and Gran popped her head out.

"Come and see this," she said. "You won't believe it!"

Mandy and James rushed to the

door with Grandad following. Blackie was sitting in the middle of the kitchen floor.

"What is it?" said James.

Then Mandy realised. Blackie wasn't running around or trying to chew anybody's shoe laces. He was just sitting there.

"I told him to sit," Gran said proudly.

"And he did?" said James. "Mrs Hope, you're a wonder!"

Gran shook her head and smiled. "It's all done by kindness," she said.

Mandy looked at Blackie. "Good boy," she said. "Wait till Sarah sees *this* at Pet Day!"

Blackie gave a short bark and scampered off out of the back door.

"My raspberry canes!" Grandad shouted. The four of them pelted after Blackie, until Mandy, flushed bright red, caught him and gathered him up into her arms.

"What that young fellow needs is a collar and lead!" Grandad said.

Mandy looked at her grandad. "But he's so young," she said.

Grandad was firm. "Fourteen weeks isn't too young for a collar and lead," he said. "You're going to be able to take him out for walks soon. You'll need to have him on a lead then."

"That's right," said James.

"Mrs McFarlane at the post office had some lovely dog collars in last week," said Gran.

Mandy smiled at her. "Then that's where we'll go," she said. "We'll do that this afternoon."

The post office was Mandy's favourite shop in the village. You could get almost anything there – comics and sweets, books and jigsaws. The shelves were piled high with all kinds of things.

Mandy pushed open the door and she and James went inside.

"Well," said Mrs McFarlane. "What can I do for you two?"

Then she saw Blackie in James's arms. "My, my," she said. "What a beautiful puppy!"

James beamed with pleasure as Mrs McFarlane came round from behind the counter to admire Blackie.

"We want a collar and lead for him," said Mandy.

Mrs McFarlane smiled. "And I have just the thing," she said. "I've got a beautiful red leather one that would just suit this little chap. And I can make him a tag with your address and phone number on it, James."

She took a collar and lead down from a hook and handed them to James.

"They're lovely," Mandy said.

James looked at the collar doubtfully. "It won't hurt him, will it?" he said.

Mrs McFarlane shook her head. "Not a bit," she replied. "It would hurt him a lot more if he got away from you and ran in to the road and got knocked over."

"That's true," said Mandy.

James made up his mind. "We'll take them," he said.

Mandy helped him fasten the collar round Blackie's neck and clip on the lead.

It wasn't easy. Blackie wriggled and squirmed and scratched at the collar with his paws.

"He doesn't like it," said James.

Mandy looked down at the little puppy. He was looking up at her and his big brown eyes looked sad.

"But he has to wear it," she said.

James looked at his pet. "I suppose so," he said.

Mrs McFarlane smiled at them. "He'll soon get used to it," she said. "Just you mind you keep it on him when you're walking him. He's far too young to be off the lead yet if he isn't somewhere safe."

Mandy nodded but James was still looking worried.

"Come on, James," she said. "Let's take him home and try walking him on the lead to see if he gets used to it."

But when they got back to James's house and set Blackie down in the garden, he didn't seem to like the collar at all. He kept scratching and tugging at it until James picked him up and gave him a hug.

"He really does have to get used to it," Mandy said gently. "It will take some time."

James looked at her. She could see he was upset. "Maybe the collar is too tight," he said. "Maybe if I loosened it a little he wouldn't mind so much."

"Maybe," said Mandy. "But don't

loosen it so much that he can slip out of it."

James nodded but he didn't look convinced.

Mandy knew it was very hard to train a puppy. Sometimes it seemed as if you were being cruel. But she was sure James would get used to training Blackie – and that Blackie would get used to being trained.

8

Pet Day

Pet Day seemed a long time coming. But, at last, the final day of the summer term arrived. Mandy and James arranged to meet before school and take Blackie to the big day together.

"Oh, look, there's Jill with Toto," Mandy said as she and James came through the school gates. Jill was carrying her tortoise in a small cardboard box with an airhole cut in to it.

Blackie was scampering about, twisting his lead round James's legs.

"Heel!" said James, pulling on the lead.

Blackie looked up at him and sat down on James's trainers.

James sighed. "I don't think we'll ever be able to train him," he said.

Mandy laughed. "Of course we will," she said. "He's only four months old." She looked up. "Here comes Jill!"

Jill waved and rushed up to them. "Look how well Toto looks, Mandy," she said. Then she saw Blackie. "Oh, James, he's gorgeous!"

Blackie stood up and wagged his tail so hard he nearly overbalanced. James swelled with pride. "I know," he said. "You'd never believe how much he's grown in the last few weeks. He was tiny when I first got him."

"He still isn't as big as Sooty," said a voice behind them. Mandy turned round. Sarah was standing there with a

al black Labrador puppy in her arms.

"Hello, Sooty," Mandy said, tickling the puppy under the chin.

"Look, Blackie," James said to his puppy. "That's your brother!"

Sarah looked at Blackie. "Your *big* brother," she said.

Mandy looked from Blackie to the puppy in Sarah's arms. "I don't know about that," she said. "They look pretty much the same size to me."

"And they're so alike," said Jill. "Don't go getting them mixed up. You wouldn't be able to tell them apart!"

"*I* would," said James. "I'd know Blackie anywhere."

"And so would I," said Mandy.

Sarah sniffed. "As if anybody could mistake my perfect little puppy for James's," she said, sweeping past them. "His was the runt of the litter!"

Mandy looked at James's face.

"Don't take any notice of her," Mandy said.

"She's probably just jealous of Blackie's

78

lovely red collar and lead," said Jill. "Her puppy hasn't got a collar. She'll have to carry him everywhere."

James looked more cheerful. "We've already started to train Blackie," he said.

"Does he know any tricks?" asked Jill.

"Not really," said James. "But he's still very young."

Mandy smiled. That was better. Poor James had looked really upset before. Sarah was the kind of person that you couldn't stand up to.

"Come on," Mandy said. "Let's go and see everyone else's pets. I can't wait!"

Mandy looked round the classroom. The walls were covered in posters of animals. There was a big display in the corner with photographs of everyone's pets and a table full of animal books. All around her, people were sitting with their animals in their cages or baskets or boxes.

There was Jill and Toto, of course. Then Peter with Timmy, the terrier. There were several rabbits, two guinea-pigs, three hamsters and a budgie. There was a hedgehog, a gerbil, two cats, four kittens, and a canary. And Gary Roberts was giving a talk about keeping snakes. Mandy was in heaven!

"It'll be your turn soon," she whispered to James.

James turned to her. "*Our* turn, you mean," he said. "I'm not standing up in front of everyone on my own. I'd be far too nervous."

Mrs Todd and Mrs Black had joined their two classes together. Everyone who had brought a pet was giving a little talk about looking after their animals.

Gary had a snake draped over his arm. He held it up to let the class see the pale yellow stripes on its greenish-black skin.

"What does it eat?" asked Amy Fenton, holding on to the cage with her pet mouse in it.

"Mostly worms and tadpoles," Gary said.

Amy looked suspicious. "Not mice?" she asked.

80

Gary shook his head. "No," he said. "Garter-snakes don't eat mice."

"And you're sure he isn't dangerous?" said Amy.

"No, of course he isn't dangerous," Gary said to Amy. "He's a garter-snake, not a python or a cobra."

"Amy is worried about Minnie," whispered Mandy, looking at Amy's mouse.

James smiled. "She should look out for Richard Tanner's cat then," he said.

Mandy looked across the room at Duchess, Richard's enormous Persian cat.

"She really suits her name," Mandy said as Duchess yawned and gazed round the classroom as if she owned it.

"Thank you, Gary," Mrs Todd said as he went to sit down. "Now, I see we have two little puppies here today." She smiled at James and Sarah. "Who's going to go first?" she asked.

"I will," said Sarah eagerly. "I want to show you what Sooty can do."

Sarah carried Sooty out to the front of

the class and put him down on the floor.

"Sit!" she instructed the puppy.

The puppy gave a short bark and wagged his tail. He didn't make the slightest move to sit.

"See," said Mandy. "Blackie isn't the only disobedient one."

"Sit!" Sarah said again to Sooty.

Sooty lay down and rolled over to have his tummy tickled.

"Oh, isn't he lovely?" said Amy Fenton.

Sarah looked round the class. "He *can* do it," she said. "He *can* sit when I tell him. Sit, Sooty!"

Mrs Todd smiled. "I'm sure he can do it, Sarah," she said. "But he's probably over-excited with all the other animals here today."

Sarah looked really upset as she bent to pick Sooty up. Mandy felt sorry for her.

"Blackie is just the same," she said.

"That's right," said James. "He does just as he likes, whatever we say!"

Sarah looked round. "Does he?" she said. "Really?"

"You bet," said James.

"Tell everyone about the cream buns," said Mandy.

"Yes, tell us about the buns, James," said Mrs Black. "That sounds interesting."

James stood up and told the story about Blackie and the cream buns. Mandy looked at him, amazed. Usually James was quite shy. But he soon had the whole class laughing. Even Sarah cheered up.

"I thought you were too nervous to

talk to the class," Mandy whispered as he sat down.

James blushed. "I *was*," he said. "But I forgot all about that when I started talking about Blackie."

The bell rang for the end of school and everyone groaned.

"My goodness," said Mrs Todd. "I've never seen you all so disappointed that it's time to go home. *Especially* on the last day of term!"

"Maybe we should do this more often," Mrs Black suggested.

"Oh, can we? Please!" said Mandy.

Mrs Todd looked at her. "You would have animals in the classroom every day if you could, Mandy," she said.

Mandy nodded. "That's right!" she said. "This is the best day I've ever had at school!"

James almost had to drag Mandy away.

"Oh, just a moment," she said. "I haven't said hello to Carrie's budgie. He was really sick last year. Just look at him now!"

James shook his head. "Do you know *all* the animals here?" he said.

Mandy turned to him in surprise. "Yes, I suppose I do," she said. She smiled. "You're right, James. There isn't one of them I don't know. They've all been to Animal Ark at some time or another."

James grinned at her. "You've got more animal friends than anybody I know," he said.

Mandy nodded, her eyes shining. "I may not have a pet of my own," she said, "but I've got a whole village full of animal friends."

In a way she was lucky. Her friends might each have a pet but she had *lots* of animals to care for.

"You know, James," she said, "I don't think I mind at all not having a pet!"

James laughed as Timmy, Peter's cairn terrier, rushed across the playground and jumped up at Mandy's legs.

"Everybody else's pets come to you," he said.

"Oh, Timmy," said Mandy, bending down to pat the little dog.

James clipped Blackie's lead on and adjusted his collar. Then he pointed a finger at the little puppy.

"Heel!" he said.

Blackie put his head on one side and looked at James curiously.

Mandy giggled. "Isn't he adorable?" she said.

James grinned. "Yes, he is," he said. "But he isn't very obedient."

Timmy padded over to Blackie and gave a sharp little bark. Blackie backed away. James kept a hold on his lead.

"Timmy is only trying to make friends, Blackie," James said to his puppy.

Blackie looked at the other dog. Then he took a step forward and nudged the terrier with his nose. Timmy snuffled gently and laid a paw on Blackie's back. Blackie gave a soft growl and butted Timmy playfully.

"There," said Mandy. "They're playing!"

There was a shout from the other side

of the playground and Mandy turned
to look.

"My rabbit! Catch him, quickly," a
small girl shouted.

"Crikey!" said James. "Laura Baker's
rabbit has escaped!"

Timmy the terrier gave a short sharp
bark and shot out of Mandy's reach. He
raced across the playground, heading
straight for the rabbit.

"Oh, no," said James. He cupped
both hands round his mouth. "Timmy!"
he called.

"James!" said Mandy. "Watch out!"

But it was too late. James had let go of Blackie's lead and the little puppy was off across the playground before Mandy or James could do a thing. The lead trailed behind him as he scampered after his new friend. Blackie obviously thought this was a game.

"Oh, no," said James. "Quick! After him, Mandy!"

9

Catch that rabbit!

Mandy and James raced across the play-ground. Blackie was well away by now. Mandy lost sight of him as the other children began to chase after Laura's rabbit. The playground was in uproar.

"Timmy! Come back!" yelled Peter, running across the playground.

He was in such a rush, he didn't see

Sarah hurrying towards the school gates with Sooty in her arms.

"Watch out!" Mandy yelled.

But it was too late. Peter and Sarah collided and Sooty jumped out of Sarah's arms. The little puppy stood for a moment, then scampered off across the playground and disappeared amongst the crowd.

Peter barely noticed. He ran on, trying to catch up with Timmy.

"Oh, catch him, catch Sooty!" Sarah shouted as Mandy came up to her. She turned to Mandy. "What if Sooty gets lost or someone steps on him?"

"Don't worry. We'll get him," said Mandy. "Blackie has run off as well."

Sarah looked really cross. "I don't care about Blackie!" she said. "It's Sooty I'm worried about." She looked at her watch. "Mum will be here in a minute to collect me. She'll be furious. She hates it if I keep her waiting."

Mandy looked at Sarah's angry expression. She was only concerned about her own pet and being late for her mum. She didn't care about anyone else.

"Come on!" James shouted as he caught up with Mandy. "I think I saw Blackie heading for the dustbins."

"It was probably Sooty," said Sarah. "Let me see." And she dashed off.

By this time the playground was full of people rushing to and fro, trying to catch the loose pets.

Mandy and James ran right round the school and into the yard on the other side

where the dustbins were.

"There's Timmy!" Peter cried and launched himself after the terrier. "Catch him," he yelled to a group of children. They fanned out, forming a half circle. Peter made a dive for Timmy and caught him up in his arms.

"Got you!" he said.

"There's the rabbit," said James, darting behind a dustbin.

"Careful, James," Mandy shouted. "Don't frighten him or he'll panic."

But James was hot on the trail of Laura's rabbit. He cornered it in the bricked-off area that housed the dustbins.

"Don't scare him," Mandy said.

James looked at her.

"Maybe you'd better do this," he said.

Mandy knelt down very quietly and held her hand out to the terrified rabbit. The little animal looked at her, its eyes huge with fear.

"There now, Nibbles," Mandy said softly. "There's nothing to be afraid of."

The rabbit wiggled his nose, sniffing

the air, then he took a tiny step towards her. Just at that moment a small black puppy scampered into view.

"Blackie!" yelled James and the rabbit's ears pricked up.

Mandy moved fast, gathering the rabbit into her arms before it could make another dash away. James tried to catch the puppy. But Sarah was there before him.

"That isn't Blackie," she said, scooping the puppy into her arms. "It's Sooty. Anyone can see *that*!"

Mandy was busy soothing the frightened rabbit.

Laura came up to her, tears running down her face.

"Oh, Nibbles is all right, isn't he?" she said. "He isn't hurt?"

Mandy smiled at her. "He's just a bit frightened," she said. "He'll be fine once you get him home."

Laura took the rabbit carefully from her and headed for the school gates.

Mandy turned to James. "Poor

Nibbles," she said. "He got the fright of his life."

But James wasn't listening. He was staring at Sarah.

"How can you be so sure that's Sooty?" he said.

Sarah looked at him scornfully. "Because Blackie had a collar on," she said. "And this puppy doesn't."

Mandy looked at the puppy in Sarah's arms. It certainly looked like Blackie.

"Blackie?" she said.

The little puppy gave a short bark and scrabbled his paws against Sarah's sleeve.

Sarah turned and began to walk away. "I tell you this is Sooty," she said.

Mandy frowned. The puppy did look like Blackie. But maybe Sarah was right. After all, she should know her own puppy! Besides, Blackie had a collar and Sooty didn't.

"Sorry!" she called after Sarah. "It's just that they're so alike."

Sarah sniffed. "I thought you said you would be able to tell the difference," she called back. "You're supposed to know so much about animals."

Mandy flushed. "I've never said that," she said quietly.

There was the sound of a car horn tooting and Sarah ran off towards the school gates and her mum's car.

Mandy looked around. The playground had cleared. Everyone had found their pets now. Only Mandy and James were left.

Mandy turned to James. He was biting his lip.

"I'm *sure* that was Blackie," he said.

"But Blackie had a collar on," said Mandy.

James looked at her. "I loosened his collar earlier on," he said. "I thought it was too tight."

"So he could have slipped out of it?" said Mandy. "Oh, James, why didn't you say?"

James looked really worried. "Sarah seemed so sure of herself," he said. "I don't *know* if I'm right. I just *think* I am. She rushed off so fast I didn't really get a chance to look at the puppy properly."

Mandy felt sorry for him. Sarah always thought she knew best. She was always so sure she was right that she made you believe her.

Mandy looked around. "So where's Sooty?" she said. "If that really *was* Blackie then Sooty must be around here somewhere. All we have to do to solve the puzzle is to find the other puppy. Once we have both, we'll be able to tell the difference easily enough."

James saw something lying in the corner of the playground.

"Look," he said, going over and picking it up.

"Blackie's collar and lead!" said Mandy.

"It looks as if I might be right," said James. "Sarah must have taken the wrong puppy home with her."

"That isn't so important at the moment," said Mandy. "At least we know that *one* puppy is safe."

"What do you mean?" said James.

Mandy turned to him, her eyes worried. "James, it doesn't matter which one it is. There's a puppy missing and we have to find him!"

10

A frightened puppy

"Where should we start looking?" James said.

Mandy bit her lip.

"I don't know," she said. "I only hope he hasn't managed to get out of the playground."

James looked worried. "Maybe he's hiding somewhere."

Mandy nodded. "If he's scared that's probably what he'd do," she said.

"Well, he isn't behind the dustbins," James said.

Mandy's eyes went to the corner of the yard. There was a heap of old floorboards and shelves piled up against the side of the bicycle shed. The workmen had put them there when they were working on the school.

"Look at all that stuff the workmen are throwing out," she said. "You don't suppose he's crawled in there?"

"We could have a look," said James.

Mandy and James ran over to the pile of rubbish. "Oh, I do hope he isn't in there," Mandy said. "It doesn't look at all safe."

"Listen," said James. "Do you hear something?"

Mandy shook her head.

"I'm sure I heard a sound," said James.

Then Mandy heard it too — a tiny squeak. But it wasn't coming from inside the pile of rubbish.

She frowned. "It sounds like it's coming from up there." She pointed to the top of the pile.

James looked up, just as a small black face appeared over the edge.

"There he is!" said Mandy.

James swallowed. "But how on earth did he get all the way up there?" he said.

"Frightened animals do the oddest things," Mandy said.

The puppy looked down at them. He put out a paw. The board he was standing on tipped forward slightly.

"Oh, no!" said Mandy, the breath catching in her throat.

"Go back!" James called to the puppy, gesturing with his hands.

The puppy backed off a little but soon stepped forward again, scrabbling at the edge of the board. He barked down at them.

"He's frightened," said Mandy. "He wants to come down."

"But that plank doesn't look too steady," said James. "If it tips over, he'll

fall right into the middle of the pile. He'll get hurt."

Mandy frowned. She looked at the pile of rubbish. It was built up against the corner of the bike shed where it met the wall that ran round the school yard. The puppy had backed away to the far side of the pile – almost against the wall.

"What are you thinking?" asked James.

Mandy looked at the sloping roof of the shed. "If I could get on to that roof I could walk along the wall and try and reach him," she said.

James looked at the wall that ran along behind the shed. "But it's too narrow," he said. "You'd fall. We'd better try and get help."

Just then the puppy put out a paw and the plank he was on rocked dangerously.

"There isn't time," Mandy said. "You've got to help me, James. I can't get up on the roof on my own."

James looked doubtful.

"Don't worry," said Mandy. "I'll be really careful."

"All right then," James said.

Mandy walked towards the shed and James came after her.

"Cup your hands," said Mandy. "Then I can stand on them and climb up on to the roof."

Mandy put her foot into James's cupped hands. "Now lift," she said as she pushed herself up.

James gave his hands a jerk and Mandy scrabbled at the edge of the shed roof. For a moment she thought she was going to fall, then she got a grip on it and heaved herself up.

"So far so good," she said as she wriggled her way on to the roof. She looked down at James.

"Be careful," he pleaded.

Mandy smiled. "Oh, I will be," she said. "If I'm not careful I won't be able to rescue the puppy."

Then she walked across the roof and on to the wall. Slowly, carefully, she balanced her way along the wall until she was just opposite the puppy. He turned his big brown eyes towards her.

"It's all right," she said to the puppy. "Nobody is going to hurt you. Come along now, come to Mandy."

The puppy looked soulfully at her. He was quivering with fright. Mandy held her hand out to him, speaking softly but firmly. The little dog began to edge towards her along the plank – away from the dangerous end of it.

"That's right," said Mandy. "Just a few steps more. Come on."

The puppy took another step. He was almost within reach. Mandy wanted to stretch out and grab him, but she knew that would be the wrong thing to do. If she missed, the puppy would panic and lose his balance. Mandy looked down at the heap of jagged floorboards and shelves and old cupboard doors. She shook her head. She wasn't going to risk it.

The little animal took another step nearer. Mandy held her hand steady. She talked to him all the time in a soothing voice, encouraging him.

"Not far now," she said.

He was almost at her hand. He pressed his wet nose into her palm and sniffed. He gave her hand a little lick.

"Good boy," said Mandy. "Come on, you can do it."

At last, after a long pause, the puppy stepped forward and nuzzled Mandy's sleeve.

Mandy put out both hands and clasped him firmly to her.

"There," she said, gathering him up. "Now you're safe!"

The puppy looked up into her eyes and Mandy frowned. This *had* to be Sooty. He just didn't feel like Blackie.

"Sooty?" she said.

The puppy gave a soft bark as if he recognised his name. But he still seemed a little frightened of Mandy.

Mandy walked very carefully back along the wall and handed the puppy down to James. The little animal yelped and began to scrabble at James's chest, trying to get down.

"That settles it," said Mandy. "This one *must* be Sooty. He doesn't recognise you at all."

"No, he doesn't," said James. "He's trembling with fright."

Mandy slid over the bike shed roof and dropped to the ground.

James looked down at the puppy shivering in his arms. Then he looked at Mandy, his eyes worried. "Let's get him back to Sarah as quickly as we can," he said. "Blackie must think we've abandoned him. I bet he's just as upset as Sooty by now!"

11

Puppy playmates

Sarah lived at the far end of the village.

Mandy and James had nearly reached the front door of her house when it suddenly burst open and Sarah rushed out to meet them.

"Oh, you've found him!" she said, putting her arms out to take the puppy. "Oh, thank you for finding him. I was so worried." She buried her face in Sooty's soft fur. "Oh, Sooty!" she cried. "I thought you were lost. I didn't know what to do!"

Sarah cradled the little puppy in her arms and Sooty barked and began to lick her face. It was plain to see he was glad to be home.

Sarah lifted her head and looked at Mandy and James.

"Blackie is in the kitchen," she said. "I didn't understand why he was so unhappy at first. Then I realised he wasn't Sooty." She bit her lip. "You'd better come in," she said.

Mandy and James followed Sarah into the house. She led them into the kitchen. A small bundle of black fur jumped up from a basket on the floor and ran towards them, his tail wagging wildly.

"Blackie!" said James, picking him up.

Blackie's tail wagged so hard that it tickled James's chin. He giggled. "And here's Mandy," he said to the little dog.

Mandy went over and made a fuss of

Blackie. The little puppy nearly jumped out of James's arms in delight.

"I was so glad when I saw you coming up the path with Sooty," Sarah said. "And Blackie's glad too."

Mandy turned to Sarah.

"When did you realise you had the wrong puppy?" she said.

Sarah blushed. "About five minutes ago," she said. "I really *did* think Blackie was Sooty. He didn't have a collar on when I found him." She bit her lip again. "But I should have been more careful. It's just that I was in a hurry. Mum gets so cross if I keep her waiting."

James and Mandy looked at each other.

"Don't worry. It's all sorted out now," James said as Blackie tried to scramble up his chest.

"But I feel so bad," said Sarah.

"Don't," said Mandy. "Sooty and Blackie look so alike, anybody could make a mistake."

"But I should have checked," said Sarah. "Especially when you said the puppy I picked up was Blackie."

"Checked?" said James.

Sarah nodded. "Sooty has a little brown patch behind his left ear," she said. She looked miserable. "I suppose I *wanted* the puppy to be Sooty because I was in such a hurry. I expect you're mad at me."

Mandy shook her head. "No, we're not," she said. "Are we, James?"

James pushed his glasses up on his nose. "Of course we're not," he said. "I'm just glad to have Blackie back. It was awful to think he might be in danger."

"Danger?" said Sarah. "What do you mean?"

"Sooty scrambled up on top of that pile of rubbish in the playground," James said. "But Mandy climbed up and got him down."

Sarah's face went white. "Oh, no!" she said. "He is all right, isn't he?" And she looked down at the little puppy in her arms.

"Of course he's all right, Sarah," Mandy said. "Put him down and watch him run about. You'll see he's OK."

Sarah put Sooty down on the floor. She began to look a little better as she watched him scamper around her feet.

"Uh-oh," said James. "Now Blackie wants to get down too."

James set Blackie down on the floor and the two puppies immediately began to roll about, playing. They ran around each other in tight circles, growling softly.

"Tell me exactly what happened," Sarah said.

James told her. Mandy was embarrassed. "I wasn't as brave as all that, James," she said. "You're exaggerating."

But James wanted to let Sarah know what Mandy had done for her pet. When he had finished Sarah turned to Mandy. "Thank you so much, Mandy," she said. "I'm really sorry I ran off with Blackie." Sarah swallowed. "And I'm really sorry I left Sooty in danger like that."

"Or *any* puppy," said James.

Sarah nodded. "That's right," she said.

"Well," Mandy smiled, "everything is sorted out now so we'd better get going."

Sarah turned to her. "Don't go!" she said. Her face grew red. "I mean, can't you stay for tea?"

Mandy and James looked at one another. Then they looked at the two puppies chasing each other round the kitchen table. The one in front suddenly stopped and turned, rearing up on to his hind legs.

"Look at Blackie!" said Mandy. Then she frowned. "Or is that Sooty?"

The three of them laughed.

"It's just as well Sooty has a brown patch behind his ear," James said.

"They're really getting on well together, aren't they?" said Sarah as the two puppies rolled under the table in one furry black ball. She looked at Mandy and James. "I wish you *would* stay for tea," she said. "The puppies are having such a good time."

"We *could* ring home and let our parents know where we are," said James.

Mandy looked at Sarah. "If it's all right with your mum," she said.

Sarah nodded. "Of course it will be," she said. "Wait till I tell her how you saved Sooty!"

Mandy smiled. "Then we'd like to stay, wouldn't we, James?"

James nodded.

"And will you tell me everything I need to know to look after Sooty?" asked Sarah.

"Of course," said Mandy. "And I'll lend you some books."

"Oh, thank you," said Sarah. "What's the first thing I should do?"

"That's easy," said James. "Get a collar from Mrs McFarlane at the post office!"

Mandy looked down at the two puppies playing happily on the floor. They were getting on very well together.

"But whatever you do, don't get a red one," she said to Sarah. "We don't want another mix-up!"

LUCY DANIELS

Animal Ark™

Kitten
Crowd

Illustrated by Paul Howard

Hodder
Children's
Books

A division of Hachette Children's Books

Special thanks to Sue Welford

Text copyright © 1996 Working Partners Ltd.
Created by Working Partners Limited, London W6 0QT
Original series created by Ben M. Baglio
Illustrations copyright © 1996 Paul Howard
Cover Illustration by Chris Chapman

First published as a single volume in Great Britain in 1996
by Hodder Children's Books

Contents

DOES ANYONE WANT
A FREE KITTEN?
if so,
tell Katie Greene,
Class Four
or phone Welford 706354

1

A problem for Mandy

"What's the hurry, Mandy?" Mr Simpson, the school caretaker, called after Mandy Hope as she ran helter–skelter down the corridor towards the front doors.

"I've been cleaning out the gerbils," Mandy said, out of breath. "And I forgot to tell James I'd be a bit late. He'll be wondering where I am!"

James Hunter was Mandy's best friend. They always rode their bikes home together. Helping with Terry and Jerry, the class gerbils, was one of Mandy's favourite things at school. She loved animals. Being allowed to help look after the school gerbils was almost like having pets of her very own.

By the main entrance door was the school bulletin board. You could put all sorts of notices up on the bulletin board. If you wanted to sell or buy anything, that was the place to let people know.

As she passed the board, one large notice caught Mandy's eye. She stopped to see what it said.

Does anyone want a free kitten?
If so, tell Katie Greene, Class Four,
or phone Welford 706354

"That's me," a voice said behind her. "I've just put that notice up."

Mandy turned to see a girl of about eight, a year younger than herself, staring at her.

"Are the kittens yours?" she asked.

Katie nodded. "We're moving house soon and Dad says we can only take their mother, Tibby, with us," she explained.

"Why?"

Katie looked sad. "He said seven cats is too many."

"Seven?" Mandy said.

"Yes, Tibby's got six babies," Katie explained.

"Oh," Mandy said. "I see. Seven cats *is* rather a lot I suppose."

"Would you like one?" Katie looked at Mandy hopefully.

Mandy shook her head. "I would *love* one but both my parents are vets. They're too busy looking after other people's animals for us to have a pet of our own."

Katie sighed. "I just don't know what's going to happen if we can't find homes for them."

Mandy's heart lurched. She could hardly bear to think of it. Six tiny kittens with no one to love and take care of them. "Maybe I can help you," she said quickly. "I'll ask all my friends."

"Oh, would you?" Katie said.

Mandy nodded. "And Mum and Dad might know someone. I'll ask as soon as I get home."

Katie's eyes shone. "Thanks."

Mandy made up her mind there and then. She would do everything she could to help Katie find homes for her kittens.

It wasn't going to be easy. Most people Mandy knew already had a pet. But she had lots of friends in the village. Surely some of them would like a kitten.

Mandy hitched her bag on to her shoulder. She went through the main doors out into the playground. Katie followed.

"Would you like to come round and see the kittens sometime?" she asked Mandy.

Mandy's eyes lit up. She couldn't refuse an offer like that.

"Oh, yes please," she said. "I'd really love to."

"I live along Meadow Lane," Katie said. "Number 16. It's just behind the church."

"I'll ask Mum and Dad if I can come this evening," Mandy said. "After tea? Will your parents mind?"

"No, of course not." Katie shook her head.

"Could I bring my friend, James?" Mandy asked. She knew James would love to see the kittens too.

"Would he like one, do you think?" Katie asked hopefully.

Mandy shook her head. "I'm afraid he's already got a cat. And a puppy."

Katie's face fell. "Oh, I guess not. See you later, then." She ran on ahead to get her bike, then rode off towards the church.

Mandy felt full of excitement. Six tiny kittens. She just couldn't wait to see them!

2

Free to a good home

James was waiting for Mandy by the bike shed. He had a worried look on his face.

James was a year younger than Mandy (he was in the same class as Katie). He and Mandy had been friends ever since Mandy had helped him choose his puppy, Blackie, from a litter of black Labradors.

"I thought you were *never* coming," James

called as Mandy hurried towards him. He hitched his schoolbag on to his shoulder and got on his bike.

"Race you home!" he called, pedalling off.

Mandy cycled quickly to catch him up. "Wait," she said. "I've got something important to tell you."

They rode side by side as Mandy told James about Katie's kittens.

"*Six!*" James exclaimed. He took one hand off the handlebars and pushed his glasses back on to the bridge of his nose. His bike wobbled. "That's not going to be easy."

"I know," Mandy said. "But I promised to try. Will you help me, James?"

"Course I will," James said. He loved animals almost as much as Mandy.

They cycled through the small village of Welford towards Animal Ark.

Animal Ark was the name of Mr and Mrs Hope's surgery, attached to the house where they lived.

Mandy usually won the race home from

school but today she lagged behind. Her mind was still on Katie's kittens.

"Come on, slowcoach," James called.

They reached James's house and stopped outside the gate. Blackie was looking out of the front window. He always watched for James to come home and he started barking excitedly when he saw them.

"Don't forget to ask your mum and dad about the kittens," Mandy reminded James.

"OK," James said. "I won't." He pushed open the front gate and went through. "I'll see you after tea."

"Yes, see you later."

Mandy waved as she pedalled quickly off towards Animal Ark.

When she got there, Mandy dumped her bike by the surgery entrance. She dashed inside. Jean Knox, the receptionist, was on the telephone.

Mandy wandered round looking at the notice board. Her heart sank. Several other people had kittens for sale. That would make it even more difficult to find homes for Katie's.

On the table was a pile of leaflets telling people how to take care of their pets. Mandy thumbed through them. Kittens, puppies, hamsters, gerbils, budgies, bunnies . . . there were hints on how to look after almost every kind of pet you could think of. The Hopes believed it was important for people to know how to take proper care of their animals.

As soon as Jean put down the receiver Mandy blurted out. "Can I see Mum and Dad? Are they here?"

Jean looked at Mandy over the top of her glasses. "I'm afraid your dad's gone out on a call. Your mum's here, though, if you want to see her."

Mandy rushed through into the surgery. Mrs Hope was packing away some medicines as Mandy came into the room. Her red hair was tied back and she wore a stethoscope round her neck. Her white vet's coat was draped across the examining table.

"Hi, Mandy," she said. "Had a good day at school?"

"Yes, fine, thanks," Mandy said quickly. She wanted to tell her mum about Katie's kittens. Her words seemed to tumble over themselves.

". . . and they're moving very soon so we haven't got long. Oh, Mum, we've got to do something to help!"

Mrs Hope smiled gently. "Now, calm down, Mandy. This will need a bit of thought."

She finished putting the boxes away and sat down. "Six kittens. Mandy, I don't know. It is an awful lot."

Mandy hoisted herself up on the examining table. "I know, but there must be *someone* in the village who wants them," she said. "And they *are* free."

"Yes, well," Mrs Hope said. "That will help, of course."

"And I could tell people how to look after them," Mandy added.

"Yes, I know you could," Mrs Hope said.

"James is going to ask his mum and dad," Mandy told Mrs Hope.

"Good. The more people that know, the better."

"What will happen if Katie can't find homes for them?" Mandy asked. She felt suddenly afraid. She hadn't see the kittens yet but she knew they would be sweet.

Mrs Hope looked glum. "I don't know, Mandy. It's not going to be an easy task, you know. Welford's only small and most people already have pets of one kind or another."

"I know," Mandy said sadly. "That's the trouble."

"You could put a notice up in the waiting-room, if you like," Mrs Hope said suddenly.

"Oh, Mum, can I?" Mandy's eyes shone. She jumped down. "I'll do it now."

"What will you do now?" said a voice from the doorway.

It was Mr Hope. He came in and put his bag down on the table.

Mandy gave him a hug and quickly explained about the kittens.

"I see." Mr Hope stroked his beard

thoughtfully. "And Katie wants to find homes for them all?"

"That's right," said Mrs Hope. "The whole lot!"

"Another pet rescue then," Mr Hope said. His eyes twinkled as he glanced at Mrs Hope. They were both quite used to Mandy's schemes to help pets.

"Looks like it," Mrs Hope replied.

"I know Katie's family," Mr Hope went on. "Mrs Greene brought Tibby to see me a few weeks before the kittens were born. She needed some vitamin shots. I'm sure they'll be grateful for your help, Mandy."

"I know Katie will be," Mandy said. "She was so worried about the kittens, Dad. I know it's not going to be easy but I've promised I'll do everything I can," she added. "And that's exactly what I'm going to do. Starting with that notice."

Mandy ran out to the waiting-room.

"Jean, could I borrow a marker pen and a piece of white card, please?"

"What on earth for?" Jean asked.

Mandy explained quickly.

"I see." Jean opened her drawer and took out the things Mandy needed.

Mandy sat on one of the chairs. She chewed the end of the pen and looked thoughtful. What should she put? Something that would *really* catch people's eyes. She began writing:

**A WHOLE CROWD OF
KITTENS**
Six cute kittens
Free to a good home
Apply to
Katie Greene, 16, Meadow Lane,
or Mandy Hope at Animal Ark

Mandy handed the notice to Jean. "Would you pin this up on the board, please?"

Jean got a couple of drawing pins and went to pin up the card. She stood back to look.

"You're right, Mandy. It does stand out. 'A good home'," she quoted. "Are you hoping that *one* person will take the

whole . . ." She chuckled ". . . crowd?"

Mandy sighed. "It would be nice if all the kittens stayed together, wouldn't it? It's going to be bad enough losing their mother, let alone being split up from their brothers and sisters."

Jean nodded. "Yes, but I don't know who on earth is going to have enough room for six kittens."

"No," Mandy said with a sigh. "Neither do I."

3

A box of kittens

Mandy was so excited about seeing the kittens she could hardly eat her tea. She sat at the table reading the class project sheet Mrs Todd, her teacher, had given her during the last lesson.

Mr Hope peered over Mandy's shoulder. "What's that you've got there?" he asked.

Mandy explained. "We've got to keep a diary."

"That'll be interesting," her dad said.

"Yes," Mandy said. "Then we've got to read them out to the class. Mrs Todd's giving a prize for the best one."

"I'm sure you'll have lots to put in yours," Mr Hope said. "There's never a dull moment here!"

Mandy grinned. "That's true."

She packed away her project sheet. She would have to start her diary later.

By the time Mandy had changed into her jeans it was almost six o'clock. She hurried along to James's house. She ran up the front path and knocked on the door. Blackie barked and doggie footsteps came thudding up the passageway.

James's door opened. Blackie pushed past and ran out, his tail wagging furiously as he saw Mandy. He gave a loud bark and started pulling at the laces of her shoes and making growling noises. Mandy chuckled and pushed him gently away. "Blackie!"

She bent down and hugged him tightly. "Now, Blackie!" she said more sternly. "I don't want shredded laces, thank you very much!"

She took hold of Blackie's collar. "Sit!" she commanded.

Blackie ignored her. He just barked again, then ran off round the side of the house. He stopped by the rose bed and started to dig.

James dashed after the puppy and grabbed his collar. He pulled him away from the rose bed and dragged him back indoors. He shut the door quickly before Blackie could run out again.

Mandy laughed. "You're not having much luck training him, are you?"

"No, 'fraid not," James said. "But I *am* trying."

"I think you've got a lot more work to do," Mandy giggled.

"Yes," James sighed. "You're right."

"Come on, then," Mandy said. "Let's go and see those kittens."

Mandy and James made their way along

the sleepy main street and across the village green.

A big man in a cloth cap was coming the other way. It was Walter Pickard. Mr Pickard had just retired from being the village butcher. He lived in one of the tiny cottages behind the village pub.

Walter's face lit up when he saw Mandy and James coming towards him.

"Hello, you two." His voice was deep and kindly. "Where are you off to in such a hurry?"

Mandy told him. "You don't want another cat, I suppose, Walter?" she asked hopefully. She knew Walter had three cats already. Surely one more wouldn't make much difference?

Walter shook his head. "Sorry, young miss. My three young'uns get up to enough mischief already, thank you."

"Never mind," Mandy sighed. "I just thought I'd ask."

Walter waved as they hurried on their way. They went along the narrow footpath beside the church. It was a short cut to Meadow Lane.

"Here we are," Mandy said as they reached Number 16. She pushed open the gate. James followed her down the path.

The house looked rather bare and empty. There weren't any curtains at the windows. Mandy guessed they had been taken down for the move. A couple of wooden packing cases stood outside the front door. There was a pile of newspapers beside them.

Just as Mandy was about to knock, Katie

came whizzing round the side of the house on her bike.

Her face lit up when she saw Mandy and James.

"Hiya," she said. "I was just going to see if you were coming." She got off her bike and propped it up against the fence. "Come on, they're round the back."

Round the back of the house was a tumbledown wooden shed. Katie pushed open the door.

Mandy peered in. She gave a shiver. It was damp and dark inside the shed. There were a lot of garden tools stacked up against the one wall and a lawn mower in the corner. There was only one small window to let in the light. Surely the mother cat and her kittens weren't in here?

Katie bent down and pulled aside a curtain covering the front of an old cupboard.

Mandy drew in her breath. There, in a cardboard box, was a small, rather thin, black cat. Nestled into her side were six tiny bundles of fur.

Mandy bent down with a little cry. "Oh, look, James. Aren't they gorgeous!"

Two of the kittens were black and two were ginger. The other two were ginger *and* black. They all had beautiful big eyes and tiny, screwed up faces.

James knelt beside Mandy. "They certainly are," he whispered.

"Does Tibby mind being stroked?" Mandy asked, looking up at Katie. She knew you had to be careful not to upset mother cats.

Katie shook her head. "No, she doesn't mind at all."

Katie knelt down beside Mandy and James. She picked up one of the ginger kittens. "Here." She gave it to Mandy. Then she picked up one of the black ones and gave it to James.

Mandy cradled the tiny creature against her chest. It mewed softly and clung to her. It had tiny, very sharp claws.

"They're so beautiful," Mandy whispered.

The sight of the six squirming, furry

creatures with their tiny ears and perfect little kitten faces made Mandy's heart turn over.

Tibby gave a small miaow as Mandy gently put the kitten back. She picked up one of the black and ginger ones and stroked it softly. She felt the tiny bones of its head and legs.

"Are you sure they're warm enough in here?" she asked Katie anxiously. She knew how important it was to keep kittens and their mothers as warm and dry as possible. She wasn't at all sure that the cats were being looked after properly.

"I kept them indoors in the cupboard under the stairs when they were first born," Katie explained. "But Mum has had to clear it out so we brought them out here. Mum says they're all right."

Mandy bit her lip. A damp old cardboard box was hardly all right! The kittens did look healthy enough but she would have felt happier if they were indoors in a warm room.

"How old are they?" she asked.

"Nearly six weeks," Katie said. "Will that be old enough for them to go to new homes?"

"Just about," Mandy said. "Most kittens are taken away from their mothers at six or seven weeks."

Katie sighed and looked sad. "I don't know what we're going to do with them. Did you ask your mum and dad?"

Mandy put the second kitten back and stood up. "Yes, they don't know anyone off-hand. But I've put a notice on our board," she added. "Maybe someone will see it at surgery tonight."

"Oh, I hope so," Katie said. "We're moving on Saturday."

"Saturday!" James exclaimed. "We'll *never* find homes by then."

Mandy frowned at him. "Yes, we will," she said firmly. "I know we will. We've got to!"

Before they went out, Mandy tucked the blanket carefully round the mother cat and her babies. She noticed that the feed bowls by the box were both empty.

"She needs some milk," she said. She picked up a bowl. "And she should have fresh water to drink whenever she wants it."

"Oh dear, I forgot to get some," Katie said. "I had to help Mum with the packing."

"Well, you can get some now, can't you?" Mandy said. She was determined not to go home until Tibby had fresh food and water.

Mandy wanted to find homes for six *healthy* kittens, not six *hungry* ones.

Mandy and James waited while Katie went indoors to fill up the dishes.

"I don't think they're very happy in here, do you?" James said, looking worried.

"No," Mandy said, "I don't." She looked angry. "People shouldn't have pets if they can't look after them properly."

"No, they shouldn't," James agreed.

"The sooner they've got a new home, the better," Mandy added. "And it's up to us to find it for them."

"Have you asked your Gran and Grandad if they know anyone?" James asked.

Mandy shook her head. "No, but we'll pop in on the way home. Gran knows *everyone*, so maybe she'll have some ideas."

4

A brilliant idea

Mandy and James said goodbye to Katie
at the front gate.

"I'll see you at school tomorrow,"
Mandy said. "Maybe we'll have some news
about the kittens by then."

"I hope so," Katie said with another sigh.

Mandy and James made their way up
the hill to Lilac Cottage where Gran and

Grandad lived. Their car was in the drive. Grandad's bike was leaning up against the wall.

Grandad was in the garden tidying up the flower borders. He grinned when he saw Mandy and James coming up the path.

"Hi, you two." He stood up and pushed his cap to the back of his head. "Gran's baking cakes. You must have smelled them."

Mandy ran to give her grandad a hug. "Gran's *always* just baked something," she said.

"True," Grandad laughed. "She's gone mad today, though. Baked enough for an army."

"Is there a village fête or something, then?" James asked.

Grandad shook his head. "No, they're for Westmoor House, the old folks' home. One of the residents is a hundred years old this week and they're having a party."

"Wow!" said James. His eyes were wide behind his glasses. "A hundred!"

"I bet she's baked a hundred cakes,

then," Mandy said, laughing. "Let's go and see."

Gran was in the kitchen surrounded by trays of cakes and a mountain of washing up. She gave Mandy a kiss.

"Sit down, you two," she said. "I'll just finish drying up then I'll find you both some lemonade."

"We'll help, won't we, James?" Mandy took a tea cloth from its rack by the cooker.

"Oh, will we?" James had already sat down at the table and was gazing hungrily at the buns.

"Yes." Mandy took another cloth and put it in front of him. He got up with a sigh and started drying some of the dishes.

"Where have you been, Mandy?" Gran asked. She dried her hands, then went over to the fridge. She got out a jug of home-made lemonade and put it on the table.

Mandy explained about the kittens. "Why don't you have one, Gran?" she said. "They're so sweet and it wouldn't be *any* trouble."

Gran shook her head. "I'm sorry, Mandy. You know how we love going away on holiday and we'd hate to be tied down with a pet."

"I'd always look after it if you were away," Mandy said.

Gran shook her head again. "Sorry, Mandy. If you own a pet you have to be responsible for it yourself, not rely on other people."

Mandy sighed. Gran was right, of course. You *did* have to be responsible for your own pets.

She dried the last of the cake tins and sat down, her chin on her hands. "You're right, Gran. But will you ask your friends?"

Gran gave her a hug. "Yes, of course I will. Don't look so down in the dumps. Something will turn up."

"What will turn up, Dorothy?" Grandad came in and went to wash his hands at the sink.

"Homes," Mandy said. "Homes for kittens."

"Oh." Grandad reached out for one of
Gran's fresh baked biscuits.

Gran slapped his fingers. "Hands off!"
she said sharply. "There won't be enough
for the party."

"Spoilsport." Grandad smiled just
the same. He looked at the clock. "I'm
going to watch the cricket on television.
Coming, James?"

"Er . . ." James seemed reluctant
although he loved cricket. He was still
eying the cakes hopefully.

"Oh, here you are," Gran said, handing

him a chocolate bun. "And help yourself to lemonade."

"Thanks, Mrs Hope!" James said.

"Don't forget we've got to load all these into the car and take them over to Westmoor House," Gran called as Grandad disappeared into the front room. James followed, a glass of lemonade in one hand, his half-eaten bun in the other.

"I won't," Grandad called back. "Just let me know when you're ready."

Mandy still sat at the table, looking glum.

"Cheer up, Mandy," Gran said. She began packing the cakes and biscuits into tins. "How long have you got to find homes for these kittens?"

"Only a couple of days." Mandy was beginning to feel desperate. "They're moving on Saturday."

"Saturday!" Gran put a bun on a plate and gave it to Mandy. "We'd better get a move on then, hadn't we?"

"Yes," Mandy said. She took a bite of the bun. It was delicious.

"Well, I'm going to a WI meeting later

this evening once I've delivered these goodies to Westmoor House. I'll ask everyone at the meeting if you like."

"Thanks, Gran, you're brilliant!"

Gran peered at Mandy over the top of her glasses. "Well, we'll see about that. Don't count your chickens before they're hatched."

"Don't count your kittens, you mean," Mandy said.

When all the cakes and biscuits were packed away Mandy and James helped put them in the car.

"We could drop you off on the way, if you like," Grandad said. "I need to pop in to see your dad anyway, Mandy. Want a lift too, James?"

"Yes, please."

They dropped James off first. Blackie was standing with his nose through the gate.

"That puppy gets bigger every day," Gran said, waving goodbye to James.

"And naughtier," Mandy said. "See you tomorrow," she called as James went up the path with Blackie at his heels.

When they got to Animal Ark, Mrs Hope was just going out on an emergency call.

"Dad's had to go out too," she said as she came through the gate. "I was just coming to find you, Mandy."

"She can come with us, if you like," Gran said through the car window. "Then we'll stay with her until you get back."

"I'd be really grateful," Mrs Hope said. "Is that all right, Mandy?"

"Fine," Mandy said. She turned to her gran. "I'll help you unload the cakes, if you like."

"That would be a great help," Gran said.

Westmoor House was about a mile outside of the village. It was a big Victorian house which had recently been turned into an old people's nursing home. There were twenty-four residents so far.

Grandad drove up to the front door. Mandy got out and rang the bell. A woman opened the door. She was tall and slim and wore a grey suit.

The woman looked surprised to see Mandy standing on the doorstep.

"My gran and grandad have brought the cakes for the party," she explained.

"Oh, lovely," the woman said. "I'm Della Skilton, the home's manager. Pleased to meet you, Mandy."

Mandy helped Gran and Grandad take the tins through to the kitchen.

"I'm so grateful," Della said. "Our residents will really appreciate it."

Mandy looked around. There was a huge cooker at one end of the kitchen. She supposed you needed a big one when you had to cook for so many people every day.

Through the window, Mandy could see a long garden with lawns and flower beds. There were two old ladies sitting in deck-chairs enjoying the warmth of the evening sunshine.

"When's the party?" Mandy asked.

"On Friday. It's going to be a big surprise for Mrs Brown."

"I love parties," Mandy said. "Especially surprise ones."

"Why don't you come after school?"
Della said. "You could help us hand
round the food. Everyone would love to
meet you, I'm sure."

"I'd love to," Mandy said. Then she
remembered the kittens. Friday was
the day before Katie moved. Mandy
might still be busy searching for a home
for them.

"Oh . . . but I'm sorry, I'll be really
busy on Friday. I'd like to come another
day, though, if I could."

Della smiled. "Come any time, Mandy.

The residents love to see young people. Some of them don't have any families, you see. And even though they all live together here some of them feel quite lonely."

Mandy felt sad. It must be horrible not to have anyone of your own. She was lucky. She had her mum and dad, and her grandparents. She had James too and other friends at school. Then there were Blackie and Benji, Walter's cats, Tom and Jerry the gerbils and all the other animals she knew. They were her friends too.

"I'll come as soon as I can," she said. "Would that be all right, Gran?"

Gran smiled. "Yes, of course it would, Mandy. You could bring James too, I expect."

"James is my best friend," Mandy told Della.

When all the cakes had been taken inside, Della went with Mandy and her grandparents to the door.

"Have a lovely party," Mandy said. "Will there be lots of presents?"

"Oh, I'm sure there will," Della said.

When they arrived back at Animal Ark, Mandy's parents were still out.

"It must be almost your bedtime," Gran said as they went in through the back door. "You run up and get ready and I'll make you a warm drink. Then I must be off to my meeting."

"Thanks, Gran." Mandy kissed her gran then ran upstairs to change into her pyjamas. She took her big old teddy bear off the bed and gave him a hug.

Mandy's schoolbag was on the chair. She took out her project sheet and gazed at it thoughtfully. She would have a lot to write in her diary today: finding out about the kittens; going to see them; then calling at Westmoor House. She would write it before she went to sleep. Maybe tomorrow she might find homes for the kittens.

Now that really would be something to put in her diary.

Downstairs, Grandad was watching TV. Mandy went and sat on the floor by his feet. She sipped her hot chocolate. Gran made the best hot chocolate!

Mandy was still thinking about the kittens. She just could not get the sweet, furry creatures out of her mind.

Suddenly Grandad gave a great laugh at the television. "Pat-dogs!" he exclaimed. "Have you ever heard of such a thing?"

"Pat . . . what?" Mandy said.

"Pat-dogs," Grandad repeated. "They're taking dogs into hospitals and nursing homes so that the patients can pat them."

Mandy frowned. "What do you mean?"

"Well," Grandad said, "someone said that people feel much happier if they have pets to love and cuddle. So that's what they're doing. They're introducing good-natured dogs into places to make the residents and patients feel better."

Mandy drew in her breath. What a fantastic idea! *Everyone* knew how happy you felt if you had a pet to cuddle.

Mandy suddenly thought of the old people at Westmoor House. *They* would love to have a pet to care for.

Mandy's heart began to race. She'd just thought of something. If you could have pat-dogs, why not pat-*cats?*

She turned her face towards her grandad, her eyes shining. "Grandad," she said. "I've just had the most fantastic idea!"

5

Mandy's plan

"But don't you see?" Mandy said when she had finished telling Grandad her idea. "I bet the old people would love to have pat-cats. They would make them feel *much* better."

"I'm sure you're right, Mandy," Grandad said. "The cats would be great company for the old folks. But *six*? Surely they wouldn't want the whole crowd?"

"There's twenty-four people there," Mandy insisted. "That's only a quarter of a cat each."

Grandad laughed. "I can see you've been practising your sums, Mandy Hope."

"That doesn't take much working out," Mandy said.

"Why don't you ask Della then?" Grandad suggested. "There's no harm in asking. You know what your gran always says. If you don't ask, you don't get."

Mandy jumped to her feet. "I'll ring her right now!"

Grandad got up too. "Not now, young lady. It's your bedtime. You'll have to do it tomorrow."

"But, Grandad!"

Grandad shook his head. "Sorry, Mandy. Rules: early to bed on school nights. One day won't make any difference. You'll get me shot if your mum comes home and you're still up and talking on the phone."

Mandy sighed. "OK, Grandad. I'll ring tomorrow."

Upstairs, Mandy sat in bed. She tried to start writing her diary, but she only got as far as putting "Day 1". She couldn't concentrate at all. Her mind kept wandering back to the kittens. She kept seeing them in that tatty old cardboard box. She kept smelling that musty old shed. What if Della didn't think pat-cats were a good idea after all? There were only two days left. Where else could she start looking?

The next day Mandy couldn't wait for school to be over.

She had told Mum and Dad her plan at the breakfast table. Mrs Hope had looked doubtful.

"How will they cope with six kittens?" she said. "Grown up cats are a different thing altogether. But six kittens could cause problems."

"There's a big garden," Mandy said. "They could play out there."

"Well," Mrs Hope said, "you'd better wait and see what Della says before you get your hopes up. But, Mandy . . ." She gazed at her daughter's excited face. "Don't be too disappointed if she says 'No', will you?"

"I won't," Mandy said although she knew she would be.

When it was time to go, James was waiting for Mandy by the front gate. She told him her plan as they cycled to school.

"That would be brilliant," he said.

"We could put our pocket money together and buy them a dish each." Mandy had been making plans in her head ever since she woke up. "And I'm sure Grandad will make them a big box if we ask him nicely."

"I'm sure my mum could find them an old blanket," James said. "One that Blackie hasn't chewed."

"Mum says they might not be able to cope with all six," Mandy said. "But I *would* like the family to stay together, if they can. Wouldn't you?"

"Yes." James looked thoughtful. "We could help, couldn't we? We could go there after school and feed them . . . things like that. Your mum could tell us what to do."

"I *know* how to look after kittens," Mandy said. "They need a warm bed and food and they need to be groomed every day. They need toys and . . ."

"There you are, then," said James. "No problem."

Mandy looked at him. "Della did say we could go and visit any time we like. James, you're brilliant!"

Katie was coming along the pavement as they arrived at school.

"Did anyone ring about the cats?" Mandy asked anxiously.

Katie shook her head sadly. "No. Have you found anybody?"

Mandy glanced at James. It would be better not to say anything until she had asked Della.

"No," Mandy said. "But my gran's going to ask around, and Mum and Dad."

"And my mum and dad," James added.

In class, Mrs Todd had to remind Mandy

several times that gazing out of the window would not help her learn her maths.

"What's the matter with you, Mandy?" she asked when lessons were over. "You're not yourself today."

"I'm sorry, Mrs Todd," Mandy said. "I've got a lot on my mind."

"Yes, well make sure it's school work that's on your mind tomorrow," Mrs Todd said. "Otherwise you're going to get behind. We don't want that, do we?"

"No, Mrs Todd." Mandy hung her head. She knew it would be hard to set her mind to *anything* until she had found a place for the kittens. She just couldn't wait to get home and ring Westmoor House.

Katie caught up with Mandy just as she was leaving. "No one wants the kittens," she said. Mandy could see she was almost crying. "I've asked everybody." A tear ran down Katie's cheek. "And my dad says he's going to get rid of them."

"Get rid of them?" Mandy asked in horror. "What does he mean?"

Katie shrugged. "I don't know. He just

said if they're not gone by Saturday morning he'll get rid of them."

Mandy put her arm round Katie's shoulders. "Don't cry, Katie," she said. "James and I have got a plan."

"What kind of a plan?" Katie asked.

"I can't tell you yet," Mandy told her. "But I promise I'll let you know about it as soon as I can."

"We need to do something soon." Katie wiped her nose with the back of her hand. "Or it's going to be too late." She began to cry even harder. "It's bad enough having to leave all my friends," she sobbed. "But leaving the kittens as well . . ."

Mandy took a tissue from her bag. She gave it to Katie. The little girl blew her nose loudly.

"I'd better get home or Mum will wonder where I am."

"Try not to worry," Mandy said as they went to get their bikes.

Katie sniffed again. "I'll try. And thank you for helping me so far." She looked sad as she rode off in the direction of the church.

Mandy felt very anxious as she rode home with James. It was all right telling Katie not to worry. But how was she going to stop worrying herself?

"Can't stop," Mandy said as they arrived at James's gate. "I want to call Della as soon as I can."

"Good luck," James said.

"I'll let you know what she says," Mandy called as she rushed off. "Keep your fingers crossed."

"I will!" James shouted.

Mandy skidded to a halt outside her gate and flung it open. She propped her bike up against the wall and hurried in through the waiting-room door of Animal Ark.

Mrs McFarlane from the post office was sitting on one of the chairs. She had a cage on her lap. Inside it was a green budgie with all its feathers fluffed up. It looked very upset about something.

"Oh dear." Mandy stopped in her tracks. She sat down next to Mrs McFarlane and peered at the bird. "What's wrong with Sparky?" She put her finger through the bars. Sparky ignored it.

"I don't know," said Mrs McFarlane. "He's been like this for a couple of days."

"Maybe he's lonely," Mandy suggested. "Perhaps he would like a friend?"

Mandy *very* nearly suggested a kitten then thought better of it. Budgies and kittens definitely did not mix!

Mrs McFarlane sighed. "A mate, you mean?"

"Yes," Mandy said. "Budgies live in flocks in the wild. Most people only have one but they do like having a friend."

"You could be right," Mrs McFarlane said. "I'll see what your mum says, Mandy. He's been quite content with talking to himself in his mirror up to now."

Mandy stood up. "You don't know anyone who wants a kitten, do you?"

"I've already asked," Jean Knox said as she came in from the back room.

"I'm sorry, Mandy, I don't," Mrs McFarlane said. "I don't think poor Sparky would take kindly to a kitten."

"No," Mandy said. "Neither do I."

"I'll ask my customers if you like," Mrs McFarlane offered. "Most people come in at some time or other."

"It's got to be soon," Mandy said.

"I'll do my best," Mrs McFarlane promised.

"Has anyone else seen my notice?" Mandy asked Jean.

"One or two people," Jean said. "That's all I'm afraid."

"Not to worry," Mandy said. "If I'm lucky I might find a home for them all this evening."

"Oh?" Jean raised her eyebrows. "All of them?"

"Yes," Mandy said with a grin. "The whole lot!"

Mandy dashed on through into the house. She dumped her bag in the hall and quickly looked up the number of Westmoor House. She keyed it in, tapping her fingers on the table.

"Please hurry," she muttered under her breath. "Please . . ."

But when someone did answer it wasn't Della.

"I'm afraid she's out," the voice said.

"Oh." Mandy's heart sank. Every minute was precious. Every passing hour took the kittens closer and closer to being "got rid of".

"When will she be back?" Mandy asked anxiously.

"About seven, I think," the voice told her. "Can I give her a message?"

Mandy thought it would be much better to talk to Della herself. "No," she said quickly. "I'll try later, thank you."

Mandy put the phone down with a sigh. She looked at the clock on the wall. Two and a half hours! How on earth was she going to be able to wait that long?

Mandy was sitting at the kitchen table writing her diary when Mrs Hope came in from the surgery.

Mandy looked up. "Did you find out what was wrong with Sparky?" she asked.

"He just needed a tonic," Mrs Hope said. "And you'll be pleased to know Mrs McFarlane is going to get him a friend."

Mandy smiled. "That's great, Mum."

Mrs Hope went to put the kettle on. "Had a good day at school, Mandy?"

"No, terrible," Mandy said. "I've been thinking about Katie's kittens all day."

"Have you rung Westmoor House?" her mum asked.

Mandy nodded and told her what had happened.

Mrs Hope came up with a solution. "I know," she said. "I've got to deliver some antibiotics to Syke Farm later. Why don't we call in at Westmoor House on the way?"

Mandy jumped up and gave her mum a hug. It would be *much* better to ask about the kittens in person.

"Oh, Mum, that would be brilliant! Can James come?" She knew James would hate to be left out.

"If his mum says it's OK," Mrs Hope said. "Ring and ask if you like."

James *did* want to come. He was waiting by his gate when Mrs Hope drew up later in the Land-rover. She opened the door.

"Hop in," she said.

"Thanks." James clambered into the back seat.

"I can't wait to see Della," Mandy told him excitedly. "Mum thinks pat-cats are a great idea, don't you, Mum?"

Mrs Hope nodded. "Yes, but it's Della you've got to convince, not me."

They arrived at the home just as Della pulled up in her car. She smiled when she saw Mandy.

"Not more cakes?" she said, her blue eyes twinkling.

"No," Mandy laughed. "We've come to ask you a favour."

"Oh?" Della said.

Mandy quickly introduced her mum then started to explain what they had come for. All her words seemed to come out too quickly.

". . . and you see we thought the old people would love them, didn't we, James?" she blurted out.

"Yes," James said, blinking up at Della.

Della held up her hand. "I think you'd better come inside and start all over again," she said.

When they got inside, Della took Mrs Hope, Mandy and James into her office.

"Do sit down," she said. "Now, Mandy, your friend Katie has got six unwanted kittens . . . right, now carry on."

Mandy finished the story.

"And Katie's dad is going to get rid of them," she said desperately. "Tomorrow!"

Della looked thoughtful. "Six cats."

She shook her head slowly. "Mandy, it's an awful lot."

"Maybe you could just take two," James said. "Or three . . . or . . ."

"But we would *really* like them all to stay together," Mandy said quickly. "Wouldn't we, James?"

"Yes," James agreed.

Della sat with her hands clasped together.

"It would be horrible for them to be split up," Mandy went on. "You said some of the people in here were sad because they didn't have families. I know they would understand how the kittens feel."

Della got up out of her chair. "Yes, you're right, Mandy. Well, let's go and ask some of the residents, shall we? Let's see what *they* think about having some pat-cats!"

6

A vote

Della took Mandy, James and Mrs Hope down a long carpeted corridor. There was a big room at the end. The buzz of talking and the sound of a television turned up loud came from inside.

Della opened the door and ushered them in. The room was full of people doing all sorts of things.

Four elderly gentlemen sat at a small table playing cards. In one corner several people were watching television. A very old man was asleep in a chair by the wide bay window and two ladies sat nearby reading newspapers.

Everyone looked up as they came in. Mandy felt suddenly shy as all eyes turned towards her. She reached up and gripped her mum's hand.

Della went across the room and turned down the television.

"Excuse me, everybody," she said in a loud voice. "I've got a young lady here who wants you to hear an idea she has."

Della took Mandy's hand and led her to the centre of the room. "Now, Mandy, why don't you tell everyone what you've just told me."

Mandy suddenly felt very nervous. Everyone was staring at her. One or two people began to mutter among them-selves.

Mandy threw her mum a pleading glance. Mrs Hope nodded encouragingly.

"Go on, Mandy," she said. "This is your big chance."

Her mum was right. This was her big chance. Perhaps it was her *only* chance to save six precious little lives.

She cleared her throat. "Um . . ." she began. "I was watching TV with my grandad . . ."

"You'll have to speak up, dear." A loud voice came from an old lady in the corner. "Some of us are a bit hard of hearing."

Mandy shuffled her feet. "Sorry," she said.

Then, in a bold voice, Mandy told the story of the kittens. She told everyone how she had heard about pat-dogs from her grandad.

". . . and I thought," she said when she had almost finished, "that a great big house like this *should* have some pets." She turned round to look at all the people watching her. "And all those empty laps should have a cat on them," she added as an afterthought.

Everyone laughed and clapped their hands.

"Hear, hear," said one of the old gentlemen who had been playing cards. "I used to have a black moggy. I still miss him."

"Me too," said a lady by the television. She had put down her knitting to listen to Mandy. "I'd love a pat-cat." She turned to her friend, a tiny lady in a floral dress. "How about you, Dora?" she shouted in her ear.

Dora nodded and smiled at Mandy.

"I hate cats," one of the men suddenly piped up. "Noisy and smelly. Got fleas, all of 'em."

Mandy's heart sank. Supposing other residents felt the same?

"Oh, George." Della went to sit on the arm of the man's chair. "They would be very well-behaved, I'm sure."

The old man screwed up his nose. "Hate 'em," he mumbled.

Suddenly a very old lady sitting with her legs up on a stool spoke loudly. "Well, I adore cats," she said. "So you can be quiet, George."

"Hear, hear," said someone else. "Be quiet, George, why don't you?"

Mandy felt a bit sorry for George. He was only telling everybody how he felt.

Della rose and came over to Mandy. "That's Mrs Brown," she explained. "She's the one who's a hundred years old tomorrow."

"Oh," Mandy whispered. She just couldn't imagine what it felt like to have lived for a hundred years.

"Come and meet her."

Della took Mandy and James over to Mrs Brown. She introduced them and they shook hands.

Mrs Brown had the palest, most wrinkled face Mandy had ever seen. She gazed at Mandy with kindly, pale blue eyes.

"You love animals, do you dear?" she asked in a soft, wavering voice.

"Oh, yes," Mandy breathed. "So does James."

"And so do I," Mrs Brown said. "I've had lots of pets in my time and I really miss them." She gazed up at Della. "Why don't we take a vote on it, Della?"

"Good idea." Della marched back into the centre of the room and clapped her hands. Everyone fell silent again. "All those in favour of pat-cats raise your hands."

Mandy held her breath. A forest of hands rose into the air. Mandy gave a sigh of relief. It looked as if almost everyone like the idea.

"Against?" Della said.

Two people put up their hands. One

was George, the man who hated cats. Mrs Brown frowned at him. He put his hand down sharply and began mumbling to himself.

The only other person who objected was a man whose name was Tom. He had been asleep in the corner and had only woken up halfway through the voting.

"Don't worry about Tom," Della said. "He always objects to everything." She smiled at Mandy and James. "There you are then! It looks as if your kittens have found a home."

Mandy clapped her hands together.

"Oh, thank you, Della!" Mandy looked round. "Thank you everybody!" She ran to hug her mum. "Mum, isn't it great?"

Mrs Hope looked very pleased. "It certainly is, Mandy."

James was so overjoyed he couldn't speak. He just stood and grinned.

"I know you'll love them," Mandy said to Mrs Brown.

"Yes, dear. I'm really looking forward to seeing these kittens of yours."

"They're not mine," Mandy said with a chuckle. "They're yours!"

They left the old people talking excitedly. Della went with them to the front door.

"I'm a bit worried about finding the time to look after them," she said.

"They're only six weeks old," Mrs Hope said. "They'll still need quite a bit of care."

"James and I have got it all worked out," Mandy said hastily. "We'll come up every day after school and help you. Would that be all right?"

"That would be wonderful, Mandy," Della said. "Is that all right with you, Mrs Hope?"

"I don't want you neglecting your school work, Mandy," Mrs Hope said.

"I won't, honestly. In fact helping out with the kittens could be *part* of my school work."

"What do you mean?" Della looked puzzled.

Mandy explained about the diary.

"I'll keep a *kitten* diary," she said. "When I've been up to visit them I'll write all about them and how they're getting on. I'll make a special copy for the residents."

"What a clever daughter you've got, Mrs Hope," said Della.

Mandy's mum rolled her eyes. "Yes, don't I know it!"

"When will you bring the kittens over?" Della asked.

"Tomorrow, if that's all right," Mandy said.

"Right, then, I'll look forward to seeing you. Oh, by the way," Della added. "Will they need injections of any sort?"

"They'll need injections against cat flu when they're a bit older," Mandy said before Mrs Hope had time to answer. "And they'll need some worm tablets too later on."

"Don't worry," Mrs Hope assured Della. "Bring them to the surgery when they're around three months old and I'll see to it."

"Thanks." Della opened the door for

them. "I'll make a special place for the kittens by the stove in the kitchen. Thank you, Mandy. I think you've made a lot of people here very happy."

"Thank *you*," Mandy said. "See you tomorrow!"

"'We *are* going to have an exciting day," Della commented. "A birthday party *and* six new residents."

Mandy hummed as they drove back towards the village. The sun was going down and the sky looked like a red blanket.

Mandy thought about the kittens,

curled up with their mother in that damp shed in Katie's garden. Soon they would all have a lovely new home and lots of people to cuddle them.

Mandy knew the old folks would love them all. Even George!

By the time they had called at Syke Farm it was getting dark.

"You can ring Katie as soon as we get in," Mrs Hope said as they dropped James off and headed towards Animal Ark. "She'll be as pleased as punch, I'm sure."

But when Mandy dialled Katie's number all she got was a strange tone.

Mr Hope listened. "That means the phone has been cut off," he said. "It must be because they're moving in the morning. If you go round early you're bound to catch them," he told Mandy. "It takes ages to load those furniture vans."

But Mandy's heart turned over with fear. What if they were too late? What if Katie's father had already carried out his threat?

What if he had "got rid" of the kittens before Mandy and James could pick them up?

Mandy thought tomorrow couldn't come soon enough.

7

Six missing kittens

"We're too late. They've gone!"

Mandy's hand flew to her mouth as she and James ran down the front path of Katie's house the following morning.

The house was all closed up, silent and empty. The family had left.

Blackie pulled excitedly at his head. Even an empty house was an adventure to him.

Mandy banged on the front door. The sound echoed down the deserted hall. Mandy's heart pounded. There was no one there. Now what were they going to do?

A man came out of the house next door.

"They've gone," he told Mandy and James. "Loaded the van last night and left about an hour ago."

"Did they take the kittens?" Mandy asked anxiously.

"Kittens?" the man said. Then he shrugged. "I don't know anything about any kittens."

"Let's go and look in the shed," James said.

They pushed open the side gate and ran round the path. The shed door was open.

James peered inside. "It's no good," he said. "They're not here. I wonder what they've done with them?"

Mandy sat down on the back step and burst into tears. "I don't know," she sobbed. She couldn't bear to think what might have happened to the kittens. "And what are we going to tell Della? The old people will be so upset."

James sat beside her, looking glum. Blackie had gone into the shed. They could hear him scrabbling about. Then he came out with a piece of old blanket in his mouth.

James grabbed it. "Leave!" he commanded. Blackie growled. He hung on more tightly than ever. He shook the piece of rag as if it were a rat.

"Blackie!" James said sternly.

At last Blackie let it go.

"It's the kittens' blanket," Mandy said, crying even harder.

"Maybe they've taken them with Tibby after all?" James tried to cheer Mandy up. "If they couldn't find homes for them?"

Mandy shook her head. "No. Katie said her dad was going to get rid of them. But where, that's what I'd like to know."

Blackie came to lick the tears off Mandy's cheeks. She buried her face in his soft fur.

After a while Mandy stopped crying. She stood up and squared her shoulders.

Crying wouldn't bring the kittens back. She and James would just have to go and explain to Della what had happened.

"We'd better go and tell Mum first," Mandy sniffed. "She was going to examine the kittens before we took them to Westmoor House. She'll be wondering where we've got to."

Mandy and James made their way back across the green towards Animal Ark.

The postman, Bill Ward, had just pulled up in his van outside the newsagents. He stopped there every morning to get his daily newspaper.

"You two look a bit glum," he said when he saw Mandy and James. "What's up?"

"We've lost six kittens," James said.

"Six kittens?" Mr Ward looked surprised "How on earth can you lose six kittens?"

Mandy explained.

"That's funny," Mr Ward said. "I passed John Greene's car this morning. It was right up the moorland road. I wondered what he was doing up there at

the crack of dawn. Where were they moving to, do you know?"

Mandy shook her head. "No. It was a long way away because Katie has got to go to a new school. Was there a furniture van with them?"

"No, I just saw his car heading for the moors." Bill shook his head. "Seems a bit odd to go for a spin the day you're moving house." He shrugged. "Oh, well, people are strange sometimes."

He said goodbye to Mandy and James and drove off.

Mandy watched him go with a frown on her face. She knew that narrow moorland road. It led right up to High Tor. She had been up there a few times with her mum and dad. They hadn't been going for a drive though. They had been going up there for a special reason.

She turned to James. "Quick!" she gasped. "I bet I know where Mr Greene was going."

"Where?" James called as Mandy hurried on ahead. He dashed after her, Blackie pulling at the lead.

Mandy had already reached her house. Mr Hope was in the drive cleaning the mud off his Land-rover.

"Dad!" Mandy said breathlessly. "Are you busy?"

"Not really," Mr Hope said. "I'm off duty this morning."

"Could you take us up to the Welford Animal Sanctuary, please?"

Mr Hope frowned. "What on earth for? I thought you were supposed to be collecting those kittens."

"We are," Mandy said. "But when we got to Katie's house everyone had gone."

"Gone? What about the kittens?"

"I've got a feeling Mr Greene might have taken them up to the sanctuary. Please, Dad," Mandy urged. "Can we go and see?"

Mr Hope opened the car door. "We certainly can," he said. "Hop in, you two."

Mandy's heart thudded as Mr Hope drove through the village. He headed up the moorland road towards the Welford Animal Sanctuary. The sanctuary was run by a woman called Betty Hilder. She took in all kinds of unwanted and abandoned animals. It would be just the place to take the kittens.

When they reached the sanctuary a donkey in the field next to Betty's bungalow brayed a greeting. The sound of dogs barking came from the row of kennels behind the house.

Mandy ran up the path and rang the doorbell.

"I'm here," a voice called from one of the barns.

Betty came out to greet them. "Hello, Mandy, what brings you here?"

Mr Hope and James got out of the car. They all began talking at once.

"Well," she said when they had finished. "As a matter of fact . . ." she paused in mid sentence. "Better still, come and see for yourselves."

Betty led them round to the back door. She opened it and they followed her inside. She took them through to the kitchen. In front of the stove was a cardboard box.

"There," Betty said. " Are they what you're looking for by any chance?"

Mandy's heart was in her mouth as she ran across and kneeled down. There, all curled round and sleepy, were the six tiny kittens.

Mandy let out a sob of relief. "James, Dad, it's them! Oh, thank goodness!"

James ran and kneeled beside her. "It's them all right," he said to Mr Hope. "Come and see."

Mr Hope took out one of the kittens.

It made a soft mewing noise. Mr Hope frowned. "This one's a bit thin," he said.

Betty came to kneel beside them. "Yes, they all are. I found them on the doorstep when I got up this morning. They've had some warm milk already but they'd probably like some more." She went to heat some milk on the stove.

Mr Hope was examining the other kittens.

"They are all right, aren't they, Dad?" Mandy asked anxiously. "I had the feeling they weren't being looked after very well."

Her dad nodded. "They need to put on a bit of weight. They're all healthy enough but they're going to need special care for a few days."

"Oh dear," Mandy said, her heart sinking. "Della's very busy with the party and everything."

"Della?" Betty came back with the milk. She poured it into three saucers.

Mandy and James placed the kittens, two by two, in front of them. They began lapping the milk up. Their tiny tongues flicked in and out so fast they were just a blur.

Mandy explained about Westmoor House.

"How wonderful," Betty said. "I'm so pleased the kittens are going to stay together. They're such a dear little family."

"But I don't know how Della's going to find time to give them special care." Mandy sounded worried.

"I'd look after them myself," said Betty, "but we've got a full house at the moment."

Mr Hope was stroking his beard thoughtfully. "Maybe we could have them at Animal Ark for a while," he said.

Mandy drew in her breath. Six kittens at the surgery! Six kittens for her to look after. It would be like a dream come true.

"Oh, Dad!" she cried. "Could we really?"

Mr Hope winked at Betty. "Oh, I should think so," he said. "Just this once."

Mandy felt like cheering. This had got to be one of the best days of her life.

8

Blackie solves a problem

A day or so later the kittens were well and truly settled at Animal Ark.

As a special treat Mr and Mrs Hope let Mandy keep them up in her bedroom. They had a brand-new wooden box that Grandad had made and James's mum had sent over a special blanket. The box stood against the warm radiator.

Mrs Hope found six little dishes for their milk. Mandy insisted they each had one of their own – and Mr Hope had found a litter tray for them to use while they were there.

Mandy gave all the kittens names. She wrote the names down in her kitten diary.

She called the largest black kitten "Cheeky".

"Black with a tiny ginger tip to her tail," Mandy wrote.

She studied the others. "Sam," she said

suddenly. "That's a good name too." She wrote that down. "All black," she put, "with a tiny ginger spot over one eye."

She went on gazing at the kittens. They were rolling around on her bedside rug pretending to fight. They looked full of health. Their eyes were bright and their tummies were quite chubby now and full of milk.

"Ginger," she said. "That sounds pretty good." She wrote it down. Then "Carrots" because the colour of the kitten's fur reminded Mandy of the lovely orange carrots Grandad grew in his vegetable garden.

Mandy thought about the residents of the home. She felt sure they would like the name "Carrots" too.

There were two kittens left. Both were black *and* ginger. The smaller of the two was very lively. He had already managed to climb up Mandy's quilt and on to her bed.

"I know," Mandy said suddenly. "Clown . . . that's a brilliant name for a naughty boy like you. And . . ." Then she remembered the old man at the home who said he didn't like cats. "George," Mandy decided. She wrote it down then looked at the page filled with names. "He's bound to like you if you're named after him."

Mandy went to pick up George. She gave him a cuddle and rubbed his soft fur against her cheek.

"There you are," she said feeling satisfied. "Now you've all got names. I can't wait to introduce you to your new owners."

Mandy felt a pang of sadness. She would really miss the kittens. Having them here was like having her very own pets. Then she smiled to herself. Six kittens were rather a lot. They needed much more space than her small bedroom. Della would still need help so that meant Mandy would still see a lot of the kittens and they would always be very special to her.

A few days after that Mr Hope declared the kittens were fit to go to their new home.

"We'll take them on Saturday morning," he told Mandy.

Mandy had been very busy looking after the kittens. She fed them and cleaned out their tray every morning before she went to school. She rushed home after school to feed them again. Then she had a play with them before tea. As they no longer had their mother to groom them, Mandy did it instead. She found a little soft brush and groomed their fur.

Each day Mandy checked their ears to make sure they were clean. Then she bathed their eyes gently with cotton wool.

Last thing every night, Mandy wrote in her diary. There were lots of things for her to write about. In fact, it was almost full up.

In the diary were the names and details of all the kittens. Mandy had written down what they liked to eat and what games they liked to play. She also wrote what happened each day.

On the day before the kittens were

ready to go to their new home Mandy made her last entry.

It had been six days since Mr Greene had left the kittens at Betty's sanctuary.

Mandy put . . .

Kitten Day 6

The last day at Animal Ark.

Morning: I gave Cheeky, Carrots, Ginger, George, Clown and Sam their breakfast. Cheeky pinched some of Ginger's. George pinched some of Sam's. Clown pushed his bowl under the chair and ate his there. He doesn't like the other kittens watching him eat his breakfast.

Evening: I gave the kittens a special wash and brush up. They start their new jobs as pat-cats tomorrow at Westmoor House. George was naughty. He ran under my dressing-table and would not come out. Clown climbed on my bed and got lost under the quilt. James came and almost sat on top of him. The others were good. I know I'll feel sad when the kittens have gone.

Mandy made a special copy of the diary for Della and the old people.

She hoped her diary would be one of the most interesting ones in the class. After all, who else would have had six kittens to write about?

On Saturday morning Mrs Hope came upstairs to Mandy's bedroom. She was carrying a big basket with a wire door on the front. It was a special basket for carrying cats and kittens.

All the kittens were asleep in their box. Mandy felt very proud as she gently took them out, one by one. They were all sleek and healthy. They yawned and stretched then sat up and began washing themselves. It was as if they knew they were going somewhere special.

Mandy took their blanket from the box and put it in the basket. She knew they would like to have their own blanket in their new home.

She put the kittens inside the basket. All except Clown. He had disappeared as usual.

Mandy lay on her tummy and looked under the bed. Clown was there playing with a pencil that Mandy had dropped.

Mandy stretched out her arm and picked him up. "Trust you!" she said. She kissed his tiny nose. Then she put him carefully into the basket and closed the wire door.

Mandy picked up the basket and took it downstairs. Mrs Hope followed with the wooden box.

Mr Hope was in the kitchen getting ready to go out on a call. "All set then?" he asked.

"Yep," Mandy said. She couldn't hide the sadness in her voice. "You'd better say goodbye to our kitten crowd."

Mr Hope peered into the basket. "Well, Mandy," he said. "They look splendid. You've certainly made a good job of looking after them."

"Thanks, Dad." Mandy sighed. "I'm really going to miss them."

Mr Hope gave her a hug. "I'm sure you'll still see lots of them."

Mandy managed a smile. "Yes, I know but it won't be quite the same as having them here."

Mrs Hope gave Mandy her car keys. "You'd better put the kittens in the back of the car," she said. "I've just got to check my appointments. I'll bring their box out with me."

As Mandy went out the front door with the basket, James was walking along the road with Blackie. They were going to come with Mandy and Mrs Hope to deliver the kittens.

'Hi, James.' Mandy put the basket down on the path. She gave Blackie a hug. Blackie sniffed at the basket, his tail wagging. He would have loved to play with the kittens.

"Have you finished your diary?" James asked Mandy when he had said hello to the kittens.

Mandy suddenly realised she had left Della's copy upstairs in her room.

"Yep," she said. "But I've forgotten to bring it down. Trust me!"

Mandy rushed back indoors.

Mr Hope was just leaving. "What's up?"

"I've forgotten my diary," Mandy said as she rushed past him. She ran up the stairs. Blackie jerked away from James and followed her up.

"Hey!" James scooted indoors after him.

Blackie was pounding up the staircase. The Labrador dived into Mandy's room and grabbed her old teddy bear from the chair. He began shaking it, ready for a game.

"Blackie!" Mandy was just getting the diary from her desk. James arrived looking red in the face.

"Sorry," he gasped.

Blackie ran out and raced along the landing.

Shouting, Mandy ran after him. "Leave!" she commanded when she caught him halfway through the bathroom door.

Blackie wagged his tail.

Mandy frowned and tried to sound angry. "Leave!" she said again.

Blackie suddenly dropped the teddy at her feet. She rubbed his head. "Good boy!"

"Good boy!" James gasped. "When has Blackie ever been good?"

"You must give him lots of praise," Mandy said in a knowing voice.

"What, even when he steals your things?" James said.

"No, when he gives them back." Mandy laughed. "Come on, Mum will wonder what's happened."

When they got back downstairs, Mrs Hope was still in the surgery. Mandy went to put the basket into the back of the car. It was then that she saw the door of the basket had swung open.

The kittens were nowhere to be seen!

"Oh, James!" Mandy gasped in horror.

She spun round. How could six kittens disappear in such a short time? Now what were they going to do?

Blackie was sniffing at the blanket. Then, nose to the ground, he headed off into the shrubbery.

"Quick!" James ran after him. "I bet he can smell them."

Mandy followed. They could hear Blackie snuffling around under one of the bushes.

Mandy bent down. There, playing with some dead leaves, were two of the kittens. She heaved a sigh of relief. She couldn't think *what* she would have done if they were lost for ever.

"Good boy!" she said to Blackie. She reached out and picked up two of the kittens, Cheeky and Ginger. "I've got two, James," she called.

Mandy put the kittens in the basket and shut the door firmly.

James had run down the path. "Here's George," he called, scooping the mottled kitten up into his arms. He suddenly dived to one side. "And here's Sam." Sam was sitting at the bottom of the tall tree by the gate. He had been playing with a feather he had found on the path. James scooped him up too and returned them both to the basket.

Mandy was looking round. "Thank goodness," she said. "Now . . . two more, Carrots and Clown. Oh, James, where have they gone?"

Blackie had run round the side of the house. Suddenly they heard the thud of something hitting the ground. Mandy and James looked at one another then ran round after him. If anyone could find the two missing kittens, it was Blackie.

But Blackie was standing with his paws on the dustbin. He had reached up and knocked the plastic lid off with his nose. It was one of his favourite tricks.

Mandy grabbed his collar. "The kittens won't be in there, silly," she said. She pushed Blackie forward. "Find them, please, Blackie."

Just then she heard a small miaow. She

spun round, frowning. Where on earth was it coming from?

James ran to look in the shed. The door was shut tight so he came back to Mandy.

"They won't be in there . . ." he began.

Mandy held her finger to her lips. "Shh."

Mandy heard the kitten again. The sound seemed to be coming from somewhere near her feet.

Then the dustbin lid began to move. Mandy jumped back in surprise. James stared at it, wide-eyed. The lid moved again. Blackie gave a little yelp and crept away, his tail between his legs.

Then Mandy gave a shout. She knew exactly what was making the lid move. She picked it up. There, underneath, looking dazed, crouched Carrots. The lid must have fallen on top of him when Blackie knocked it off.

"Poor old Carrots," James said.

Mandy picked up the kitten and hugged him to her. She quickly felt his

back and legs. "He's OK," she said. "Blackie, you're the cleverest dog in the world." Blackie was sitting by the hedge looking sorry for himself.

"And the naughtiest." James gave his dog a hug. Blackie wriggled out of his grasp and ran to the front gate.

They quickly searched the back garden but there was no sign of the last kitten. They hurried back to the basket and put Carrots inside.

Mrs Hope came out of the surgery door with the kittens' box.

"Sorry I've been so long," she said. "I had to take a telephone call. Come on, let's get going."

Mandy quickly explained what had happened.

"Clown's still missing," she said. "We can't possibly go until we've found him."

"He can't have gone far." Mrs Hope looked round. "Maybe he went back indoors?"

Mandy shook her head. "He couldn't have. The door's been shut all the time."

James had followed Blackie back to the bottom of the tree. Blackie looked up and suddenly began barking.

"Over here!" James shouted.

James was looking up into the branches. He pointed. "Up there," he said.

Mandy gasped. She suddenly felt wobbly at the knees. There, sitting on one of the highest branches was Clown, the naughtiest kitten of them all!

9

The best presents

"Well, well, what *have* we got here?"

Mandy turned to see Mrs McFarlane standing behind her. She was gazing up into the tree.

"A kitten," Mandy told her. "Stuck."

"Better call the fire brigade," Mrs McFarlane said. "You'll never get him down on your own."

"I think we should try first," Mrs Hope said. She went round the back to get a ladder. But when she put it up against the tree it only reached halfway.

By now, other village folk had arrived. Walter Pickard had been on his way to the shop. He stood gazing up into the tree shaking his head.

"My, my," he said. "That *is* a long way up."

Then Grandad arrived on his bike.

"What's going on, Emily?" he asked Mrs Hope.

When she told him he burst out laughing. "Mandy Hope," he said. "Whatever next!"

"It's not funny, Grandad," Mandy said, close to tears.

Grandad stood with his chin in his hand. "Maybe you could persuade him to climb down?"

Mandy shook her head. "He's too scared."

Mandy's teacher, Mrs Todd, drew up in her car. She got out to see what all the fuss was about.

"Well, Mandy," she said, when Mrs Hope explained. "This is going to be something to put in your diary."

Mandy was growing more and more anxious. Everyone was talking about Clown but no one was *doing* anything.

"I think we *had* better get the fire brigade," Mrs Hope said at last. "I'll explain to them on the phone." She disappeared indoors.

Mandy stood gazing up at Clown. He was crouched on a fragile branch looking very frightened indeed. She didn't think

225

she could bear it if he made a sudden movement and fell off. "Please, please stay still, Clown," she whispered. "We'll get you down, I know we will."

James was crouched down, his face buried in Blackie's neck. It seemed he couldn't bear to look either.

It wasn't long before the fire engine came roaring along the village street towards them. It drew up outside Animal Ark.

Six burly fire-fighters piled out.

"Right," the chief said. "Where's this kitten?"

Mandy pointed. "Up there," she said anxiously. "He's very scared. Please can you get him down?"

The chief tipped his helmet back on his head. He gazed upwards. Then he made a salute. "Don't you worry, young lady," he said. "We'll do our best."

The fire-fighters got their long ladder from the top of the engine. With a screech and a clang they put it up against the tree. Higher and higher it went, until it almost reached the branch where

Clown was crouched. One of the fire-fighters began to climb. When he got to the top he stretched out his arms.

Mandy held her breath. The fire-fighter's fingers were centimetres away from Clown. The kitten gave a small miaow and moved backwards.

By now, quite a crowd had gathered. Everyone gave a gasp.

Then the fire-fighter shook his head and began to climb back down.

"I'm sorry,' he said when he reached the bottom. "That branch is too fragile to hold my weight. I'm not sure we're going to be able to get him."

Everyone began talking among themselves.

"We'll have to call for a longer ladder," the chief was saying. "I can't risk one of my men having an accident."

Mandy stared up at Clown. It could be ages before another ladder arrived. She had to *do* something. If the branch wouldn't hold the fire-fighter's weight, maybe it would hold hers?

Mandy looked at James and held her finger to her lips. His mouth fell open when he saw what Mandy intended to do. James began to shake his head. "Mandy, no!" he hissed.

Blackie lay down and hid his face in his paws.

But Mandy had made up her mind. She was going to rescue Clown herself.

She began to climb the ladder. Up and up until she felt she might almost touch the sky. She didn't dare look down. Right at the top she stepped carefully on to Clown's branch.

"Now don't move," she told him sternly. "Stay where you are and I can reach you."

Mandy clung on for dear life. Her heart was thudding like a drum. She crawled slowly along the branch towards the kitten. Then she stretched out her hand and scooped him up. The kitten clung to her, glad to be rescued at last.

Below, Mandy heard Mrs Hope shout. "Mandy, what on earth are you doing!"

She had been talking to Grandad with her back to the ladder and had only just noticed what Mandy was up to.

But Mandy was already on her way down. When she reached the bottom everyone cheered.

Mrs Hope took hold of her arm. "Mandy, you shouldn't have done that. You might have fallen!" She looked angry.

Mandy hung her head. Now she was back down, she realised just how dangerous her climb had been. "I'm sorry, Mum. I couldn't leave poor little Clown up there any longer."

Mrs Hope put her arm round Mandy and gave her a hug.

"Don't you ever do anything like that again," she said.

Soon Clown was tucked safely back in with the other kittens.

Mandy thanked the fire-fighters. She watched as the fire engine roared off down the main street. It wasn't every day that there was an exciting rescue in the sleepy village.

* ★ ★

When the kitten basket was safely in the back of the car they set off for Westmoor House.

"You'd better leave Blackie in the car," Mrs Hope told James when they arrived at Westmoor House. "He'll only cause havoc. We've had enough trouble for one day!"

"OK." James wound down the window a little so that Blackie had some fresh air.

One of Della's helpers opened the door. "Come in, come in," he said. "Everyone's waiting."

Mandy felt excited as they marched along the hall towards the big sitting-room at the end. She and James carried the basket between them. With six chubby kittens inside it was quite heavy.

In the sitting-room everyone stopped talking and turned to look at them. One man went to turn off the television.

"Hurrah!" someone called. "They're here!"

Mandy smiled and nodded. Della rose

from a chair by the fire and came over.

"We've all been so excited," she said. She peered into the basket then drew in her breath. "Oh, they're so sweet! Look, everyone!"

Mandy put the basket down. She opened the door a fraction and took out one of the kittens.

"This is Sam." She took him over and gave him to a lady sitting by the window.

Then she took out another one. "This is Carrots," she announced.

Everyone smiled and laughed. "What a good name," one of the men called. He held out his arms. "Can I hold him?"

James took Carrots and placed him in the old man's arms.

"I've got a cat too," James whispered.

"What's his name?" the old gentleman asked.

"Benji," said James. "He's big and fluffy. I've got a puppy as well. He's called Blackie."

"I used to have a dog," the old man told him. "But a cat will do just as well."

He smiled down at Carrots. The kitten was purring and rubbing his face against the old man's woolly cardigan.

"This is Cheeky," Mandy bent down to take the black kitten from the basket.

Cheeky wriggled and jumped out of her arms. She scampered over to Mrs Brown and began to climb up the leg of her stool. Della went to rescue her. She put her on Mrs Brown's lap. Cheeky curled up and began to purr gently. The old lady's face lit up as she stroked the kitten's soft fur.

"Thank you, Mandy," she said. "Cheeky is going to be my favourite."

"And this is Clown." Mandy lifted the kitten out. Clown seemed no worse for his ordeal in the tree. "He's *really* bad," Mandy said. She looked round. "Who wants him?"

A dozen arms were outstretched. "Give him to Tom," Della suggested.

Mandy took the kitten over to Tom. Tom was sitting with his back to everyone. Mandy tapped him gently on the shoulder. "Would you like to hold this one?" she said softly.

Tom mumbled something that Mandy could not hear.

"Please," she said. "You'll feel much better. He'll make you laugh, honestly."

The old man turned slowly. The frown fell from his face when he saw the pretty kitten.

Mandy put Clown gently into Tom's lap. Tom turned away again and softly stroked Clown's head. Mandy could see Clown was going to be Tom's best friend. She smiled to herself and went back to the basket.

There were two kittens left.

"This is Ginger," she said taking her out. Ginger was the laziest of all the kittens. She opened one sleepy eye and yawned.

"I'll have her," said Dolly.

Mrs Hope took Ginger over. The kitten took one look at Dolly then curled round on her lap and went fast asleep. Dolly smiled. She lay back in her chair and closed her eyes too.

"Now . . ." Mandy took George out. She went over to the old man who didn't like cats. "He's named after you, George," she said, gazing at the old man.

The old man shook his head and turned away. "Smells!" he said.

"No, he doesn't," Mandy said indignantly. "He's clean and beautiful. Look at him."

The old man looked at Mandy. Then he looked at the kitten. He shrugged his shoulders. "If no one else wants him . . ."

"I do," a voice came from the corner. "I'll have the little fellow."

George snatched the kitten from Mandy's arms. "No, you won't," he said. "He's mine!"

"Oh, dear," Mrs Hope said. "I hope they're not going to quarrel over them."

Della laughed. "I'm sure they'll sort it out." She turned to Mandy and James. "They're beautiful. Thank you so much, you two."

Mandy took her diary from her pocket. She gave it to Della. "This is for you," she said shyly.

Della opened the diary. As well as writing all about them, Mandy had drawn a little picture of each of the cats.

Della drew in her breath.

"It's lovely, Mandy." She took the diary across to Mrs Brown. "Look at this!"

Soon the diary was being passed around. There were "oohs" and "ahhs" from everyone.

"Did you have a nice party?" Mandy asked Mrs Brown.

"Yes, thank you, dear. It was lovely," the old lady told her.

"Did you have lots of presents?"

"Quite a few," Mrs Brown said. "But these kittens are the best present of all."

Mrs Hope looked at her watch. "I'm afraid we've got to go. I've got some calls to make."

"We'll come up tomorrow and help feed them," Mandy said as they made their way to the front door.

"That would be lovely, Mandy," Della said. "Although I've got a feeling there are going to be plenty of willing hands to look after our new family. You've made a lot of people very happy."

"No," Mandy said. "It's the *kittens* who are going to make them happy!"

On the way home, James sat in the back seat with Blackie. "You don't think they'd like a pat-puppy as well, do you?" he joked, struggling to stop the puppy from chewing the seat belt.

Mrs Hope chuckled. "Not one like Blackie, I shouldn't think. They would never cope!"

10

The winner

At school the following Monday every-one was talking about their diaries and the things they had put in them.

"I didn't have anything exciting to write," one of the boys said. "All I did was go to school, eat my dinner and watch telly."

"I went to my auntie's," someone else said.

"My brother broke his leg playing football," a friend of Mandy's told her. "So I wrote all about that."

"I went to Walton and got a new pair of shoes," another friend said.

"I went on a train through the Channel Tunnel," someone said. "It was great."

At last the time came for the class to read out their diaries. Mandy realised she had found so much to cram into hers it might take the whole lesson to read out.

When Mandy's turn came she stood up and cleared her throat.

"Kitten Diary," she said in a loud voice. For some reason she didn't feel nervous any more. "One week in the life of six kittens."

"Kitten Day 1 . . ."

When she had finished there was silence for a minute. Then everyone clapped.

Mandy blushed and sat down quickly.

"Very good, Mandy," Mrs Todd said. She looked at a boy called Paul Jackson, "Now, Paul, your turn."

When everyone had read their diaries, Mrs Todd said, "Excellent everyone. Now, I want you all to write down on a piece of paper whose diary you thought was the best."

Mrs Todd waited a few minutes then went round collecting the votes. She sat at her desk counting. Then she looked up. She had a broad smile on her face.

"The winner is . . . Mandy Hope. Well done, Mandy!"

Mandy went red as everyone clapped again.

Mrs Todd opened her desk and took out a bag. "Come and get your first prize, Mandy."

After school Mandy rushed out to show James her prize. It was a book about animals of the rainforests.

"Oooh!" James turned to a picture of a tiger. "I wouldn't like to have to look after one of those."

"I would," Mandy said jumping on her bike. "I'd love it!"

A warm breeze was blowing as Mandy and James raced across the green. The houses and shops glowed in the afternoon sunshine.

Mandy said goodbye to James at his gate and headed off towards Animal Ark.

She felt sad as she wheeled her bike up the brick path. There wouldn't be any kittens waiting for her today. Mandy knew she would miss them terribly. Then her heart lifted. She would be able to go to Westmoor House to see the kittens whenever she wanted. She knew they would be well looked after and, after all, she did know lots of pets that were *almost* her own.

Mandy pushed open the door of Animal Ark and went inside.

An envelope lay on the kitchen table. It was addressed to Mandy. When she opened it she saw it was a card from everyone at Westmoor House.

"Thank you for our pat-cats, Mandy," it said. "They are all lovely. Come and see us again soon."

Mandy sat back in the chair. She smiled to herself. There was no doubt about it. Finding such a loving home for a whole crowd of kittens had been one of the best things she had ever done.

LUCY DANIELS

Animal Ark™

Rabbit
Race

Illustrated by Paul Howard

Hodder
Children's
Books

A division of Hachette Children's Books

Special thanks to Helen Magee

Text copyright © 1996 Working Partners Ltd.
Created by Working Partners Limited, London W6 0QT
Original series created by Ben M. Baglio
Illustrations copyright © 1996 Paul Howard

First published as a single volume in Great Britain in 1996
by Hodder Children's Books

Contents

1

New arrivals

"Let's take Blackie round to Lilac Cottage after tea," Mandy Hope said to her friend James Hunter as they came out of school on Friday afternoon.

Blackie was James's black Labrador puppy. Mandy and James had house-trained him. Now they were trying obedience training. But that wasn't so easy.

"Good idea," said James. "I want to see if we can teach him to fetch. He's still a bit nervous of Benji, so it's difficult to train him at home."

Benji was the Hunters' cat. He was just the teensiest bit jealous of Blackie.

"Poor Benji," Mandy said as they walked down the main street in Welford. "I expect he feels a bit left out."

James nodded. "I know," he said. "But it won't be for long – not now your gran and grandad are letting us use their garden. It's very kind of them."

"Gran and Grandad love Blackie," Mandy said firmly. "They're happy to have him there. It's no problem."

Mandy never thought any animal was a problem – she loved them all. Both her parents were vets so she'd been brought up surrounded by all sorts of animals. James looked up at her and shoved his glasses further up his nose. He was a year younger than Mandy but he was her best friend, probably because he liked animals nearly as much as she did!

"Bye, Mandy! Bye, James!" Sarah Drummond called as she got into her mother's car outside the school gates. "Have a good weekend!"

"Tell Sooty we were asking after him!" Mandy called back.

Sarah and James had got puppies at the same time. Her puppy, Sooty, was one of Blackie's brothers.

Mandy and James waved as Sarah's mum drove off.

"Blackie and Benji will be fine together once they get used to each other," Mandy said to James.

"And once Blackie is a bit more obedient," said James.

"We'll get Gran to have a word with him," said Mandy. "She seems to be able to do anything with Blackie."

James grinned. "Look!" he said, pointing across the road.

Peter Foster, one of Mandy's classmates, was just opening his front gate. He staggered back as a hairy bundle of brown and grey fur hurled itself at him. It was

Timmy, Peter's cairn terrier.

"I wonder if your gran could do anything with Timmy," James said.

Mandy giggled. "I shouldn't think so," she said. "Timmy is something else."

They reached the post office. From here Mandy and James went different ways. Mandy lived in an old stone cottage called Animal Ark at one end of the village and James lived in a modern house at the other end.

The cottage was not just Mandy's home. Her parents' surgery was attached to it, which was where the name came from. Mandy always looked forward to going home after school to see how the animals were getting on – and to check on any new arrivals.

"See you later," James said to Mandy.

Just then there was a rumbling sound and an enormous van came trundling down the High Street and drew up outside the post office.

The driver leaned out and pushed his cap back on his head.

"Can you tell me if we're anywhere near Hobart's Corner?" he asked Mandy and James.

They looked up at him in surprise. There was another man in the cab with him. On the side of the van, in big red letters, were the words Rapid Removals.

"Oh," said Mandy. "Is somebody moving into Hobart's at last?"

The man smiled. "I don't know about *at last*," he said. "But somebody is moving in – if I can find the place."

"Oh, sorry," Mandy said. "If you go down to the end of the road and turn left, you can't miss it. It's a big old house, the gate is right on the corner."

"It's falling to bits," said James. "It's been empty for ages."

The driver looked at the other man. "Just as long as we can get the furniture in, that's all that bothers us," he said. "Thanks a lot for your help."

Before Mandy could ask him any more questions, he drove off.

A bell rang as the door of the post

253

office opened behind them.

"Now what was that all about?" asked Mrs McFarlane.

Mr and Mrs McFarlane ran the post office. Mandy always thought the post office was the best shop in the village. It sold comics and sweets and all kinds of things. Mandy and James had even got Blackie's first collar and lead there.

"Somebody is moving into Hobart's Corner," said Mandy.

Mrs McFarlane looked surprised. "My,

my," she said. "After all this time. And I never heard a word about it! I wonder who's bought that old place." She disappeared back into the shop to tell Mr McFarlane.

James and Mandy looked at one another.

"Mrs McFarlane hears about *everything* that goes on in the village," Mandy said. "How did she miss this news?"

James shrugged. "Beats me," he said. "Why don't we go and have a look? Hobart's Corner is on the way to Lilac Cottage. I can meet you there."

Mandy ran all the way home and rushed through the door of Animal Ark.

"You'll never guess," she said.

"Guess what?" said Jean Knox, the receptionist, looking up from a pile of forms.

Mandy leaned against the reception desk and tried to get her breath back.

"A removal van stopped outside the post office to ask directions to Hobart's Corner," she said, her eyes shining.

"Someone has come to live there at last."

Jean raised her eyebrows in surprise and her spectacles slid down her nose and off the end. They swung on the chain round her neck as Jean shook her head.

"Well now, fancy that," she said. "And there was I thinking that old house would never be sold."

"I must tell Mum and Dad," said Mandy, jumping up. "Are they very busy?"

"Your dad's got a patient with him," Jean replied. "And your mum has gone to a calving up at Baildon Farm. But she said she'd be back in time to make tea."

"Oh, good!" said Mandy. "Dad tries his best but he just isn't as good a cook as Mum."

"And just what's wrong with my cooking?" said a voice from the door of the surgery.

Mandy whirled round. Mr Hope was standing there, smiling his lopsided smile.

"Oops!" said Mandy.

Mr Hope laughed. "Caught you out there, Mandy," he said.

Mandy noticed her dad was holding something small and furry.

"It's Ginny!" she said. "Is she better?"

Ginny had been a very sick little guinea-pig when she first came to Animal Ark. Her teeth were very overgrown and she couldn't eat properly.

"I've trimmed her teeth and she's eating like a horse now," said Mr Hope.

"Oh, Ginny," Mandy said, stroking the guinea-pig's reddish-brown coat. "Pam will be so pleased."

The little animal looked up at her with its big dark eyes. Pam Stanton was in

Mandy's class at school and she had been really worried about Ginny.

"Oh, Dad, I've got really exciting news," said Mandy.

She told her father all about the removal van and Hobart's Corner.

"Do you think the new people at Hobart's will have pets?" she said.

Jean Knox laughed. "Most nine-year-olds would wonder if they had children," she said.

"But our Mandy is more interested in their pets," Mr Hope said.

Mandy shook her fair hair out of her eyes. "Of course I want to know if they have any children."

Jean perched her glasses on her nose and looked over the top of them at Mandy.

"Could that be because the more children there are, the more pets there will be?" she asked.

Mandy smiled widely at both of them. "How did you guess?" she grinned.

2

Jack

"Do you see anybody?" asked Mandy as she and James peered through the tall iron gates at Hobart's Corner.

James shook his head and gave Blackie's lead a tug, trying to bring him to heel. But Blackie had other ideas. He was busy snuffling at the grass verge, searching out all sorts of interesting smells.

"I can see a car," James said. "But the removal van has gone. Blackie, behave!"

"He can't help it," said Mandy, smiling down at the gangly black puppy. "He's growing up so fast and there's such a lot for him to learn. He's interested in everything."

"I suppose so," said James, his eyes still on the house. "I always thought that house looked really spooky."

Mandy looked at the tall, dark building. The paint on the window frames was peeling and the garden was badly overgrown.

"That's just because it's been empty so long," she said. "Dad says the last person to live in it was an old army captain. He moved away five years ago to live with his daughter."

"I don't remember him," said James.

"We were only little," Mandy said. "His name was Captain Hobart. That's why this was called Hobart's Corner."

Blackie gave a muffled bark and began to scrabble at the bottom of the gate.

"What now?" asked James, picking him up.

But Mandy had seen what was attracting Blackie.

"Look," she said. "There's somebody in the garden after all. It looks like a little boy."

"Where?" said James.

Mandy pointed. "Sitting in that apple tree," she said. "He's watching us."

Mandy raised her hand and waved. "Hi, there!" she called. "What's your name?"

The boy continued to look at them but he didn't speak.

"Maybe he didn't hear you," said James.

Mandy shook her head. "He heard all right," she said. "He just didn't answer."

Just then a woman came round the side of the house. She was dressed in faded jeans and a baggy jumper and her hair was tied back with a scarf. Her face was streaked with dust.

"Oh, hi!" she said as she saw Mandy and James at the gate. "You haven't seen a little boy, have you?" She looked worried. "I told him not to go out of the garden. The gate wasn't open, was it?"

Mandy shook her head and pointed at the boy in the apple tree. "Is that him?" she said.

"Oh, there you are, Jack!" said the woman. "You gave me a fright, disappearing like that." She smiled at Mandy and James then turned back to Jack. "Come down out of there. You've got visitors."

Jack scrambled down out of the tree and stood for a moment looking at Mandy and James. He looked about six or seven years old. Mandy drew in her breath when she saw his face properly. He had been crying.

"I don't want visitors," he said. "I hate this place. I didn't want to come here. Leave me alone!"

And with that, he raced off across the grass and disappeared round the side of the house.

Mandy and James looked at the woman, embarrassed.

She smiled at them and drew a hand across her forehead. It left a long, dusty streak.

"Oh dear," she said. "I wonder if this move was a good idea after all. Jack isn't happy about it."

Mandy and James looked at each other. It was difficult to know what to say.

"He'll get used to it," Mandy said at last, "once he makes friends. Welford's a really good place to live."

The woman smiled. "I hope so," she said. Then she looked thoughtful. "He's going to start at the village school on Monday," she said. "I hope he'll be all right."

James smiled. "We go there too," he said. "Tell Jack he's come at a good time. We've got the school picnic at the end of this term. That's always great fun."

"And we'll keep an eye on Jack at school if you like," said Mandy. "Until he settles in."

The woman looked really grateful. "Thank you. That would be terrific," she said. Then she looked round. "I must go and find him. Goodness knows where he'll have got to now." She turned away, then turned back. "I forgot to ask your names," she said.

Mandy and James told her and she smiled. "I'm Mrs Gardiner," she said. "Jack is seven – he's usually the friendliest little boy. I just hope he gets over this." She looked at Blackie at James's side. "But I don't expect seeing your puppy helped. Oh dear, we've got such a lot of work to do."

Mandy and James watched as she walked away over the grass.

"She seems nice," said James.

Mandy nodded. "But Jack is really unhappy," she said. "Did you notice he'd been crying?"

"And what did she mean about Blackie not helping?" said James.

Mandy shrugged. "We've got a lot to find out about the Gardiners," she said. "And I know the perfect place to start."

"Where?" said James.

"Gran!" said Mandy. "If she doesn't

know something about the Gardiners, then nobody will!"

Gran and Grandad were working on their vegetable patch when Mandy and James arrived.

"Now you keep out of my beans, young Blackie," Grandad said, leaning down to give Blackie a pat.

Blackie looked up at him and gave a short bark.

"I don't know whether that's a yes or a no," Gran said. She looked at Mandy and James. "You two look as if you're bursting with news."

Mandy picked up a hoe and began to weed between the lines of beans.

"It's the new people at Hobart's Corner," she said. "They've got a little boy but he seems really unhappy."

Gran nodded and leaned on her own hoe.

"I went round there this afternoon with a flask of tea and some scones," she said.

"Nobody ever gets to move in round

here without a plate of your Gran's scones to help them along," Grandad said with a wink.

"You know how it is," said Gran. "People can never find the kettle no matter how carefully they packed it."

"And what did you find out about the Gardiners?" Mandy asked.

Gran shook her head. "They've taken on a lot of work with that house," she said. "They're hoping to turn it into a country guest house."

"But Hobart's Corner is falling to bits," said James.

Grandad nodded. "It seems Mr Gardiner is going to do it up."

"Wow!" said Mandy. "That'll take forever."

"And that isn't their only problem," Gran said. "Little Jack didn't want to move in the first place, especially just after his dog died."

"What?" said Mandy, looking up from her hoeing.

Gran nodded. "It was really sad," she

said. "He had a dog called Fred but Fred got very ill and died just before they moved here."

"That's rotten," said James, looking down at Blackie. He bent down and gave the dog a cuddle. "I know how I'd feel if anything happened to Blackie."

"That explains why Mrs Gardiner said seeing Blackie would upset him," said Mandy. "Oh, poor Jack. No wonder he's so unhappy."

Gran looked at her. "Maybe you could try to make friends with him," she said.

Mandy nodded. "Of course we will," she said.

"But we can't force him to be friends," said James. "He doesn't seem to want us around."

Mandy looked thoughtful. "What if Jack had another pet?" she said. "Nobody could be unhappy if they had a pet to look after."

Grandad looked doubtful. "It might be a hard job replacing Jack's dog," he said.

Mandy shook her head. "I wasn't thinking about replacing Fred," she said. "I was just thinking about Jack having a new kind of pet."

"Like what?" asked James.

Mandy frowned. "I don't know yet," she said. "I'll think about it. I'll have to find out what Jack is like."

"How will you do that if he won't even talk to you?" said James.

Mandy shrugged. "I'll think of a way," she said. "Once he has a pet to care for, a pet that will love him back, he'll be much happier. You'll see."

3

Animal antics

Mandy craned her neck, trying to see down to the front of the school assembly hall.

"Who are you looking for?" whispered James.

Mandy turned to him. It was Monday morning. She had been thinking a lot about little Jack over the weekend.

"I'm looking for Jack," she said.

"Remember, we said we'd keep an eye on him."

"And we will – if he'll let us," said James.

The juniors were lined up at the front of the hall.

"There he is," said Mandy. "Look, he's talking to Laura Baker."

James smiled. "Maybe he's made a friend already," he said. "Laura is really nice. She's all excited just now because one of her rabbits is having babies."

Mandy nodded. "Fluffy's babies are due any day," she said. "Maybe she's telling Jack about it."

But James shook his head. "Maybe she is but Jack doesn't seem interested. Look. He's stopped talking now."

Mandy watched as the little boy's head drooped. "He looks awfully sad, James."

James nodded. "We'll make sure we see him at breaktime," he said. "And we'll try to cheer him up."

Just then Mrs Garvie, the teacher, called the room to attention.

"As you know we will be having

the school picnic at the end of term," she said. "And I want you all to think of a theme for the day. I'm looking for suggestions." Her eyes twinkled. "Though we've had so many over the years I don't know if you can come up with anything new."

The pupils of Welford Village School had a picnic on Beacon Hill every summer and every year there was a different theme. Last year it had been pirates and they'd had games like 'walking the plank' and 'tug of war'.

Mandy stuck her hand in the air and waved it frantically.

Mrs Garvie looked at her. "Have you got a suggestion, Mandy?" she asked. "Already?"

Mandy nodded. "Oh, Mrs Garvie," she said. "Can the theme be animals? We've never had that one before."

Mrs Garvie smiled. "Animals!" she said. "I might have known that's what you'd come up with. It sounds a splendid idea, Mandy."

Mandy flushed with pleasure as James clapped her on the back.

"Great idea," he said.

"What do the rest of you think?" asked Mrs Garvie.

There was a general murmur of approval from the rest of the pupils.

"I think it sounds terrific," said Peter Foster. "Can I bring Timmy?"

Mrs Garvie gave him a look. "So long as you don't let him off the lead, Peter," she said. "We all know the mischief Timmy can get up to."

"Can we have a go-kart race at the picnic?" Andrew Pearson said. "Beacon Hill is great for go-karts."

Andrew was in Mandy's class. His older brother had helped him make a go-kart last half-term. It started a craze and now quite a few of the kids in the village had go-karts. James had been talking about getting his dad to help him make one.

Mrs Garvie looked doubtful.

"That depends, Andrew," she said. "How many people have go-karts?"

Half a dozen hands shot up into the air, Peter's among them.

"Pam Stanton's got one," said Mandy, looking across to where Pam was waving her hand wildly in the air.

"I wish I had a go-kart," James said. "I'd love to enter the race."

Mandy looked at him. "I thought your dad was going to give you a hand making one," she said.

James nodded. "He is," he said. "But we haven't got round to it yet. Dad's been really busy at work. He hasn't had time."

"I could help you," Mandy said.

James smiled. "Thanks, Mandy," he said. "But I wouldn't even know where to start. And Dad says if I have a go-kart it has to be safe."

Mrs Garvie counted the upraised hands.

"Oh, well," she said. "That's plenty of competition for a race. I think we can have a go-kart race."

"What's that got to do with animals?" Jill Redfern said.

"We can give the go-karts animal names," said Andrew.

Jill grinned. "Peter can call his the *Terrier*," she said.

"Lucky for you, Jill, you haven't got a go-kart," said Peter. "You'd have to call it the *Tortoise*."

Jill stuck out her tongue. She had a pet tortoise called Toto.

Mrs Garvie coughed and gave them a look.

"Sorry, Mrs Garvie," said Jill.

"But Andrew's idea is a good one," said Mandy. "We can have all kinds of animal races. Like hedgehog races where you have to roll."

"And snake races where you have to slither," said Jill.

"I'll bring Gertie," said Gary Roberts. "She can show you how it's done."

Gary Roberts had a pet garter-snake called Gertie.

"Can we have a rabbit race?" piped up a voice.

Mrs Garvie looked down at little Laura Baker.

"Of course we can, Laura," she said. "You ask Mandy about it later."

Mandy turned to James. "We could use sacks for the rabbit race, so that people would have to hop," she said.

"What?" said James and Mandy knew he was still thinking about the go-kart race.

Mrs Garvie looked at the assembled pupils. "You've got a lot to think about," she said. "Let Mandy have your ideas and don't forget we'll need a name for the day as well."

They always had a name for the picnic day. Last year it had been Pirate Playtime.

"Animal Antics!" said James and then blushed. James didn't usually call out during assembly.

People took up the name and began repeating it as they filed out of the assembly hall.

"Animal Antics," said Mandy to James as they separated to go to their classrooms. "That's a terrific name."

James looked pleased. But he still wasn't as cheerful as usual. Mandy watched as he walked away down the corridor, wondering how she could help.

"Mandy, Mandy, can we really have a rabbit race?" said a voice at Mandy's elbow.

Mandy turned and looked down at Laura Baker. Laura was seven years old. She had dark curly hair tied up on top of her head with a big red bow. Jack Gardiner was with her.

"Hi, Laura. Hello, Jack," Mandy said. "Sure we'll have a rabbit race, Laura. How

is Fluffy? Has she had her babies yet?"

Laura beamed. "Not yet," she said. "But she's fine. It won't be long now."

Mandy looked at Jack. The little boy looked terribly unhappy.

"How are you getting on, Jack?" she asked.

Jack looked up at her. "OK," he said in a dull voice.

"I've got to look after him," said Laura importantly. "He's in my class and he's going to sit beside me."

Mandy smiled at the little girl. "I'm sure you'll look after him very well, Laura," she said.

"Come on then, Jack," said Laura. "We'd better hurry or we'll be late." And Laura sped off down the corridor.

Mandy looked at Jack. Then she looked around. Everybody else had gone.

"Look, Jack," she said quietly. "I heard about Fred."

Jack's big blue eyes filled with tears.

Mandy put out a hand and touched his shoulder.

"Wouldn't you like another pet?" she said.

Jack looked up at her and blinked the tears away.

"I'll never have another pet," he said. "And I'll never like living here."

Mandy looked at him sadly. She understood how lonely he felt. Suddenly a voice called down the corridor.

"Hurry up, Jack!" Laura yelled. "You don't want to be late on your very first day."

Jack turned and marched away. Mandy sighed. First James and now Jack. What was she going to do about them?

4

A surprise for James

Mandy sat at the kitchen table in Lilac Cottage on Tuesday afternoon, swinging her legs and thinking.

"And how is little Jack Gardiner getting on at school?" asked Mandy's gran.

"How did you know I was thinking about Jack?" Mandy said.

Gran's eyes twinkled. "Magic!" she said.

Mandy grinned, then she looked serious. "I've tried to cheer him up," she said. "But he just doesn't seem to *want* to like Welford."

"What about him getting another pet?" said Gran.

Mandy shook her head. "He doesn't want to know," she said.

"Perhaps it's just too soon," said Gran.

"Maybe," Mandy said doubtfully. "But don't you think if he had a pet to look after he would feel so much better?"

Gran smiled. "I'm sure you're right," she said. "Now cheer up and drink your orange juice. I've got work to do in the garage and you can help me."

Mandy raised her glass to her mouth and finished her drink.

"There," she said, wiping her mouth. "That was yummy. And those ginger biscuits! You really *are* magic, Gran."

"My special recipe," said Gran, opening the kitchen door. "But you still don't look very cheerful."

"Oh, I've got another problem," said

Mandy as she followed her gran down the path to the garage.

"What's that?" said a voice from the garage. "Did you say you had a problem, Mandy?"

Mandy peered into the garage. Dust danced in the sunlight in the doorway. She shaded her eyes.

"Is that you, Grandad?" she said.

Grandad poked his head out from behind a pile of boxes.

"It certainly is," he said. "In here up to my ears in junk."

"That isn't junk, that's *jumble*," said Gran.

Grandad looked at her and pushed his hat back on his head. "It's jumble to you, Dorothy," he said. "But it's junk to me. Look at this."

He pulled a pram out from behind an old wardrobe.

Gran looked at it. "Well, maybe you're right about that," she said. "It *is* past its best."

Grandad let out a whoop of laughter. "Past its best?" he said. "It was Mandy's pram. Look at it! It's falling to bits."

Mandy looked at the pram. "I can't imagine I was ever little enough to fit in there," she said.

Grandad grinned. "You weren't too little to wreck it," he said. "You never did like being strapped into a pram, Mandy."

"Don't listen to him, Mandy," Gran said. "You were a lively baby, that's all."

Grandad chuckled. "That's one way of putting it," he said.

"The wheels are all right," Mandy said, examining the pram.

Grandad looked at them. "I remember when your dad was a boy," he said, turning to push the pram out of the way. "I showed him how to make a fine go-kart out of a set of old pram wheels and a couple of wooden boxes."

Mandy's head shot up. "What?" she said. "What did you say, Grandad?"

Grandad looked at her in surprise. "What's the matter?" he said.

Mandy was nearly dancing with

excitement. "Could you do it again?" she said. "Could you make another go-kart?"

Grandad scratched his head. "I reckon I could," he said, looking puzzled. "I didn't know you wanted a go-kart."

Mandy shook her head. "Not for me," she said. "For James." And she told Gran and Grandad all about the go-kart race.

Grandad smiled when she had finished.

"Tell you what," he said. "You and James collect all the bits we need and I'll help you make the best go-kart in Welford."

"What kind of things do you need?" asked Mandy.

Grandad thought for a moment. "A couple of strong wooden boxes," he said. "Or, better still, some fresh wood. I've got sandpaper but we'll need some paint. We've got the wheels." He looked at Mandy's old pram. "And I reckon we could use the bottom of the pram to make the base out of. It's a good, solid one. I might even be able to fit the brake to the go-kart."

"What about my old bike?" said Mandy. "It's got brakes.'

"That might do," said Grandad. "Then all we'd need is a guide rope. It's amazing what you can make out of a few bits and pieces. I used to build some great go-karts when I was a boy."

"And you'll help James?" said Mandy.

Grandad laughed. "I'd love to," he said. "It'll be just like old times. I can hardly wait for the two of you to collect up the stuff."

Mandy shook her head. "Oh, I'll collect all the stuff myself," she said. "I want it to be a surprise for James. Just wait till I present him with everything he needs! What do you think he'll say?" She looked at her gran and grandad. "You know what," she said. "You're *both* magic!"

She grinned up at Gran and Grandad. That was one of her problems solved. Now all she had to do was solve the other one.

Mandy was so deep in thought as she cycled past Hobart's Corner that she didn't notice the small figure sitting astride the garden wall.

"Wood, rope, paint," she muttered to herself.

"Hello," said Jack.

Mandy looked up, surprised. "Oh, hello, Jack," she said, coming to a stop. "I didn't see you there."

"You were talking to yourself," said Jack.

Mandy smiled at him. This was the first time he had spoken to her first.

"Can you keep a secret?" she asked.

Jack's eyes lit up with interest for a moment. "What kind of secret?" he said.

"The surprise kind," she said. And she told him about the go-kart for James.

"That sounds great," said Jack, his eyes shining.

Mandy was amazed. For the first time she saw him happy. He looked like a different person.

"So now I'm going to go round the village collecting everything I need," she said.

"Where are you going to try?" said Jack.

Mandy thought for a moment. "I should get wood from Amy Fenton's dad at the timberyard," she said. "Then I thought I might try Laura's dad for nails. He was making a nesting box for Fluffy last week so he must have some."

"Fluffy?" said Jack.

"One of Laura's rabbits," said Mandy. "She must have told you about Fluffy. She's going to have babies soon."

Jack nodded. "Yes, she did," he said,

kicking at the garden wall.

Mandy stopped as an idea suddenly occurred to her. All of the people she planned to visit had pets.

She looked at Jack. He wasn't interested in another pet. But what if he *saw* some pets? He might change his mind. It was worth a try.

"Of course all this stuff is going to be awfully heavy," she said with a sigh. "I don't know how I'm going to manage it all on my own."

Jack looked at her. She could see him trying to make up his mind.

"Do you want some help?" he said at last.

Mandy smiled. "Oh, Jack, that would be really good," she said. "Would your mum let you?"

"I'll ask her," said Jack. "When do you want to go?"

Mandy bit her lip. She didn't want to give Jack a chance to go off the idea.

"Now," she said firmly. "Everyone will be at home."

"OK," said Jack. "I'll run and ask Mum."

Mandy hugged herself, crossed her fingers, turned round three times for luck and danced with impatience until Jack got back. If her plan worked, Jack might – just might – be back tonight asking his mum another favour.

"I've got to be home by six," Jack said as he came running back to the gate, pushing his bike.

Mandy beamed at him. "No problem," she said. "We should have everything sorted out by then."

5

Visiting

Mandy and Jack's first call was at Amy
Fenton's house.

"Amy's dad runs the timberyard on
the Walton road," Mandy said as she and
Jack cycled up Welford High Street.
"That's a good place to start if we're
looking for wood."

Jack nodded. "Amy Fenton," he said.

"I haven't met her. Is she in your class?"

"She's in James's class," Mandy replied. She cast a quick sideways look at him. "She's got a pet mouse called Minnie."

Jack cycled on, his eyes straight ahead.

"Here we are," Mandy said. "And there's Amy in the garden."

She braked and leaped off her bike, waving to Amy.

"Amy," she called. "We've got a really big favour to ask."

Mandy explained what she and Jack were looking for and Amy went to get her dad.

"Come and see Minnie while you're waiting," she said.

Mandy smiled. She hadn't even had to ask.

"You'll love Minnie," Mandy said to Jack as Amy took them into her bedroom and went off to get her dad.

Jack looked at the little white mouse in its cage. It pushed its tiny pink nose up against the bars, twitching its whiskers and looking at them with bright eyes.

Mandy gently opened the cage and took Minnie out, letting her run up and down her arm.

"You hold her, Jack," she said.

But Jack shook his head. "I think Amy's coming back," he said, turning away.

Mandy sighed. It wasn't going to be easy getting Jack interested in another pet.

"Great news," said Amy coming in to the room. "Dad says he can let you have some offcuts. He'll deliver them to Lilac Cottage tomorrow if that's OK."

"Brilliant!" said Mandy. She giggled as Minnie scampered up her arm and tickled the back of her neck.

"And Mum says Aunt Julia has loads of old tins of paint lying around in her garden shed," Amy finished.

"Even more brilliant," Mandy said. "We'll go round there right now."

Mandy sighed. Amy's aunt Julia was Richard Tanner's mum. And Richard Tanner had a Persian cat called Duchess. If Jack didn't like mice, maybe he would like cats better.

But Jack didn't seem to like Duchess any more than he had liked Minnie. The Persian cat stalked through the garden in front of them as they made their way out to the shed.

"Isn't she beautiful?" said Mandy, bending to stroke the cat's long silky fur.

Jack stretched out a hand to Duchess but the cat must have sensed his reluctance. She backed away from him. Jack drew his hand back quickly.

"She won't hurt you," Richard said.

"I don't like cats much anyway," said Jack.

Richard nodded. "That must be it," he said. "Cats know when people don't like them."

Mandy sighed as she watched Duchess flick her tail and disappear behind the garden shed. But they *did* come away with four half-full tins of paint.

The next house they tried was where Gary Roberts lived. Gary wanted to be an inventor when he grew up so his bedroom was always full of junk – or so his mum said.

"Gary's bound to have something useful," said Mandy.

While Gary searched through his bedroom cupboard, Jack inspected Gary's garter-snake, Gertie. Mandy held her breath. He looked really interested. Gertie slithered towards him, her green and yellow body gleaming. She raised her head slightly, her tongue flicking in and out. Jack and Gertie stared at each other. Maybe Jack would like a *snake*, Mandy thought.

"I knew I had one of these somewhere," Gary yelled from the depths of the cupboard.

There was a honking sound and Jack whirled round, Gertie forgotten.

Mandy put the snake back in her tank and looked at the rusty old-fashioned motor-car horn in Gary's hand.

"Oh, thanks, Gary," she said. "That's going to be really useful."

Jack took the horn and turned it round. The rubber bulb was almost worn through in places and the metal clip was rusted.

"This is great," he said, grinning at Mandy.

"Don't mention it," Gary said. "Any time! Now I thought I had a steering wheel in here somewhere."

"Don't bother, Gary," Mandy said hastily. "The horn is enough."

Mandy was almost in despair as they packed the horn into her bicycle basket alongside the tins of paint.

"What else do we need?" said Jack.

Mandy looked at her list. "Rope," she said. "I wonder where we could get that?"

"I could chop a bit off Mum's washing-line," said Jack.

Mandy gave him a look. "And get into trouble?" she smiled. Even if she wasn't being very successful with this pet idea, Jack was certainly friendlier than he had been before.

"I know," he said. "Laura said she got a new skipping-rope yesterday. Maybe she would let us have her old one."

"Good idea," said Mandy. "Let's go."

Laura met them at the door, her face flushed with excitement.

"Oh, you'll never guess," she said. "Fluffy is having her kittens – right now!"

"Now?" Mandy breathed. "Oh, Laura, that's wonderful. How is she? How many kittens are there so far?"

"Kittens?" said Jack, puzzled.

"That's what you call baby rabbits," Laura said. "Come and see. But don't make a noise. Fluffy has been in a hutch on her own since she got pregnant and she's used to everything being really quiet."

Mandy and Jack followed Laura through to the conservatory where Mr Baker had set up a separate hutch for Fluffy. Pregnant rabbits had to be on their own because, as well as needing extra feeding, they had to start nest building. And they couldn't do that in a hutch with other rabbits.

Mrs Baker was already there, kneeling down in front of the hutch. She put her fingers to her lips as the children came in.

Mandy and Jack crouched down with Laura between them and gazed at the black-and-white doe. The nesting-box was inside the hutch. It was a simple open-sided box with fresh hay bedding. Mandy could see that it was lined with soft fur. She new that Fluffy would have plucked fur from her belly to line the box so that her babies would have a soft bed to lie on.

Then Mandy forgot everything else as she caught sight of Fluffy's babies – tiny

furry little things. They lay there, snuggled into Fluffy's body, their eyes tightly closed.

"Ugh!" said Jack. "They're all wet!"

"Sshh!" Laura whispered. "If you disturb her she might get frightened and she might eat her babies. We must be very quiet."

Mandy held her breath as Fluffy stretched and began to breathe more heavily. Her huge dark eyes rolled towards Mandy as she strained to give birth.

"Come on, Fluffy," Mandy whispered under her breath. "Good girl, you can do it."

Then there was another baby, and another. At last, Fluffy relaxed.

"Five," Laura whispered as Fluffy bent her head to her babies. "Do you think she's finished?"

Mrs Baker nodded. "It looks like it," she said quietly. "Look at the way she's licking her kittens now."

Laura turned a shining face to Mandy and Jack. "Oh, wasn't that wonderful?" she said. "And all her babies look just fine."

Jack was looking at Fluffy and her babies, his face lit up in a way Mandy had never seen before.

"Oh," she said. "Wasn't that the best thing you ever saw? Look at the little rabbits. They're so tiny and helpless."

"They can't see or hear yet," said Laura. "Their eyes won't open for another ten days."

Mrs Baker smiled. "They've got their mother to look after them for the next two months. They'll depend on her for milk," she said. "After that we'll have to find homes for them."

Jack turned to her. "But who will you give them to?" he said.

"To people who will love them and care for them," Mrs Baker said. "Maybe even someone like you."

"Me?" said Jack as if he couldn't believe it. "You mean I could have one of Fluffy's babies?"

Mandy looked at Jack, her eyes shining. Mrs Baker examined Jack's eager face.

"Oh, please, Mummy," said Laura. "I can tell Jack all about looking after rabbits."

"Are you used to looking after pets, Jack?" Mrs Baker said. "They can be a lot of work, you know."

Jack flushed and Mandy held her breath.

"I used to have a dog," he said. "But he died. I'd like another pet now."

Mrs Baker looked from Jack to Laura to Mandy.

"I just know Jack would love his pet," Mandy said.

Mrs Baker smiled. "Then why don't you ask your parents?" she said to Jack. "If they say yes then you can be the first to choose, Jack. You can have the pick of Fluffy's litter."

Jack's face blazed with happiness. "I'd like that," he said. "I'd like that a lot."

Mandy felt the smile spreading over her own face. Success!

When they got back to Hobart's Corner Mrs Gardiner was just coming out of the kitchen door into the garden. Jack skidded his bike to a halt and raced across to her.

"Mum, Mum!" he yelled as he ran. "Laura says I can have one of Fluffy's baby rabbits if you'll let me." He stopped in front of his mother, looking up at her.

"A baby rabbit?" Mrs Gardiner said. "A new pet?"

Jack bit his lip. "I know you're really busy but it wouldn't be any trouble," he said. "It's just a *little* rabbit."

Mrs Gardiner smiled. "I think we could manage to give a little rabbit a home," she said. "So long as you promise to look after it."

Jack's face lit up. "Oh, I will, Mum," he said. "So can I really have a rabbit for a pet?"

Mrs Gardiner looked across the top of Jack's head at Mandy. Then she crouched down in front of Jack and put her arms round him.

"Of course you can, Jack," she said. She looked into Mandy's eyes, smiling. "I think that's a wonderful idea."

6

Getting ready

The following afternoon Mandy, Gran, Grandad and James were standing in the driveway of Lilac Cottage. Blackie was busy wrapping his lead round James's ankles. James had his eyes shut.

"OK, you can open your eyes now," Mandy said to James.

James opened his eyes and looked at the

pile of things on the floor of the garage.

Blackie pulled at his lead and sniffed at a pot of black paint. Then he sneezed and shook himself.

"What's all this?" asked James.

"Guess!" said Mandy.

James looked puzzled. "It looks like a heap of junk to me," he said.

Mandy put her hands on her hips and looked at him. "Well, James Hunter," she said, "it might look like a pile of old junk to you *now*, but once you and Grandad have finished with it, it's going to be the best go-kart in Welford. At least that's what Grandad says." And she turned to look at her grandad.

"That's right," said Grandad.

James was standing there with his mouth open. "A go-kart?" he said. "You mean we're going to make one?"

Mandy laughed. "Not me! Grandad's the expert," she said.

"But you're going to help," Grandad said to James.

James turned to him, his face shining.

"Oh, Mr Hope, this is terrific." He looked at Mandy. "Where did you get all this stuff?"

"Oh, here and there," said Mandy. "And I've got more news for you. Jack wants one of Laura's baby rabbits."

"No kidding," said James. "How did you manage that?"

Gran smiled. "Come inside and get a cold drink and Mandy can tell you all about it," she said.

"And then we'll draw up the plans for the go-kart," Grandad said.

"Oh, and Grandad," said Mandy, "could you please help Jack to make a rabbit hutch? There's plenty of wood here. Jack's mum and dad are so busy with all the work at Hobart's Corner they won't have time."

Grandad pushed his hat back and scratched his head. "And I thought I was supposed to be retired," he said. He looked at James. "Come on, lad," he said. "Let's have our break before the whole of Welford starts queueing up for carpentry work!"

James looked at Blackie. "But what about Blackie?" he said. "We were going to have a training session this afternoon."

Mandy took Blackie's lead. "Just you leave Blackie to us," she said. "Gran and I are going to train him."

James laughed. "Do you hear that, Blackie?" he said. "You'd better be on your best behaviour."

Blackie looked up at him and put his head on one side.

"And don't try looking pathetic," Gran said to the little animal. "It's all for your own good."

Blackie lay down, put his head on his paws and sighed.

Gran shook her head. "That puppy might not be the most obedient dog in the world," she said. "But I swear he understands every word you say to him."

"Biscuit!" Mandy said to Blackie.

The puppy was up on his feet at once, trotting beside her, tail wagging.

"It looks as if you're right, Gran," she said. "Now all we've got to do is to try and get him to do the things he *doesn't* want to do."

Grandad and James spent the next week working on the go-kart. James couldn't talk about anything else.

"Your grandad taught me how to use a saw," he said proudly on the way to school one morning. "And he showed me how to cut dovetailed joints."

"What are those when they're at home?" Mandy asked.

James tried to explain but Mandy couldn't follow him.

"Come and see it," said James. "It's looking really great."

So, that evening, Mandy went round to Lilac Cottage with James.

"Wow!" she said when Grandad wheeled the go-kart out of the garage. "That looks great. Are those really my old pram wheels?"

Grandad smiled. "They look a bit different now, don't they?" he said.

"You can say that again," said Mandy,

staring at the long, low wooden structure perched on its wheels.

James ran his hand over the smooth wood of the go-kart. "Those are dove-tailed joints," he said, pointing to the deep box seat at the back of the go-kart.

Mandy looked closely. The side of the seat was joined to the back almost like a jigsaw.

"Now we have to fix a footboard and guide rope to the front," said James.

"A what?" said Mandy.

"It's a bit like a steering wheel," said Grandad. "Or a tiller on a boat."

"Oh, right," said Mandy. She grinned. "Tell you what," she said. "I reckon this is going to knock spots off Andrew's go-kart."

"You bet!" said James.

Grandad looked at him. "Ready?" he said. "We've still got a long way to go if this is going to be the best go-kart in Welford."

James picked up a hammer and a handful of nails. "You bet!" he said again, laughing.

After that, Mandy went round every

evening to Lilac Cottage. She was soon involved in helping with the go-kart – and Jack's rabbit hutch.

The rabbit hutch was coming on, but a bit more slowly than the go-kart. Grandad had built a sturdy frame on legs. It stood about a metre off the ground. Grandad was letting Jack do as much as he could and Mandy could see that Jack was loving it. Each evening after tea he raced straight round to Lilac Cottage to work on the hutch.

Jack was as keen on carpentry as James was but Grandad liked someone to keep a close eye on him. So Mandy soon got into the habit of working with Jack.

With Grandad's help, they had glued and nailed the sides of the rabbit hutch together. Then they fitted the partition between the two compartments inside the hutch and, finally, got ready to attach the roof to the sides.

"The roof has to overhang the hutch," Grandad said. "You don't want the rain to get in – or cats either."

"Would cats hurt a rabbit?" Jack asked.

Grandad took a roll of chicken wire and measured a length off it against the front of the hutch. "A cat would kill a baby rabbit," he said. Then he looked at Jack's concerned face. "But we're going to make your hutch cat-proof!"

7

The Cheetah

Two days later, James's go-kart was almost finished.

"There," James said proudly from the driveway. "It just needs some paint now. What do you think of the go-kart, Mandy?"

Blackie gave a short bark and leaped up at James's chest.

"Sit!" said Mandy and to her surprise, Blackie sat and looked up at her.

Mandy gave him a pat, making a fuss of him for being a good dog, and looked at the go-kart. It sat outside the garage at Lilac Cottage, the spokes of its wheels polished and sparkling in the sun. "It's terrific!" she said.

James beamed and even Grandad looked proud.

"I'm pretty pleased with it myself," he said, looking at the finished product. There was an open-ended box mounted on the back with a seat built into it. Mandy looked at the long piece of wood with a crossbar on the end that stretched from below the seat to the front of the go-kart.

"What's that?" she said.

James got into the go-kart and sat on the seat.

"It's for steering," he said, putting his feet on the crossbar and pushing. "It's like a kind of rudder."

Mandy watched as the front wheels

turned from side to side.

James picked up the looped rope that was lying across the front of the go-kart.

"And that's the guide rope," Grandad said. "James can control the go-kart with his feet and his hands."

"Wow!" said Mandy. "You're a genius, Grandad."

Grandad laughed. "You're a bit of a genius yourself," he said, looking down at Blackie who was sitting quietly by Mandy's feet. "You've certainly got Blackie well on the way to being the model puppy."

Mandy laughed. "Gran's the one who's really good with him," she said. She turned to James. "What animal are you going to name your go-kart after?" she said.

James stuck a hand in his back pocket and pulled out a picture he had cut out of a magazine. It was a very large cat with a reddish-yellow coat broken up by solid black spots. There were stripes running from the corner of its eyes down the sides of its nose.

"It's a cheetah," she said.

James nodded. "Did you know that the cheetah is the fastest animal in the world?" he said. "There are records of them running at speeds of up to 114 kph. So, if I've got the fastest go-kart, it ought to be named after the fastest animal."

"We can paint it in cheetah colours," said Mandy. "I've got some black paint and we can mix red and yellow to get the base colour. James, your go-kart is going to be the smartest in Welford."

Grandad pointed to the tins of paint piled up at the side of the garage.

"Paint and brushes," he said. "You two get on with it."

The gate at the bottom of the back garden opened and Mandy looked up. Jack was coming up the path with his mother.

"And here's my other apprentice carpenter," Grandad said smiling. "Hello, Mrs Gardiner. How are you settling in?"

Mrs Gardiner came up the path towards them. "I think we're getting there," she said. "But there's such a lot of work to do. I just came to thank you for all your help building this hutch with Jack."

Mandy grinned. "Grandad is loving it," she said. "Aren't you, Grandad?"

Mr Hope laughed. "I certainly am," he said. "Your Jack is going to turn into a fine carpenter."

Jack beamed with pleasure as Mandy turned to him.

"Hi, Jack!" she said. "Where have you been? You look like you've got good news."

"Hoppy opened his eyes today," he said excitedly. "I've just been to see him!"

"Hoppy?" said James.

Jack nodded. "That's what I'm going to call my rabbit," he said.

"Lovely!" said Mandy. "What colour is he?"

"Black and white," Jack said. "Just like his mum."

Grandad looked at Jack. "We'd better get on with this hutch then, Jack," he said. "We want to have it ready in good time."

Jack nodded. "But it'll be another six

weeks before I can take Hoppy home," he said. "He's only two weeks old. He still needs his mother to feed him."

"He'll soon be on solid food," said Mrs Gardiner. "Then *you* can feed him."

"Laura says we can start giving him some solids when he's three or four weeks old," said Jack. "I can't wait to try feeding him. And I can't wait to take him home."

"Then let's get busy," said Grandad. "We want this hutch to be fit for a king."

"Oh, we do," said Jack. "We really do!"

Mrs Gardiner looked at him. "He's a different boy these days," she said to Grandad. "You and your wife have been so kind."

"It's a pleasure," Grandad said. "Why don't you go in and have a word with Dorothy?" His eyes twinkled. "And if she's putting the kettle on for a cup of tea, I wouldn't say no."

Mrs Gardiner laughed and walked towards the house. "I'll tell her," she said.

"Right," said Mandy, rolling up her sleeves. "I'll give James a hand with the go-kart."

When Mandy and James had finished painting, the go-kart looked even more splendid. They stood back and admired it.

"Those black markings look really good," said Mandy. She looked at the picture of the cheetah James had pinned to the garage wall. "Just like the real thing," she said.

James turned to look too. Then something scampered between them both, whizzing in and out of the paint tins. Mandy saw the yellow paint tin rock slightly, then it tumbled over, spreading a pool of paint over the garage floor.

"Blackie!" James shouted.

The puppy stopped abruptly, turned round, skidded on the wet paint and rolled over.

"Oh, no!" said Mandy. Then she started to laugh.

"What are you laughing for?" said

James as Blackie scooted off across the garden.

"Look!" said Mandy, pointing. Blackie's coat was patterned black and yellow all over. "He's like a miniature cheetah."

James shook his head. "How on earth are we going to get that paint out of his coat?"

Mandy bit her lip to stop laughing. "We'll ask Mum and Dad," she said. "They're bound to know."

"White spirit," said Jack, turning round from the hutch. He looked a little sad for a moment. "Fred once got red paint all over him. We soaked it off with white spirit and then gave him a good shampoo."

"Just make sure you don't let any of the

white spirit get in his eyes," said Grandad. "There's a bottle of it on the shelf here."

"Thanks for the tip, Jack," James said. "I'll just see if I can catch him."

Mandy walked over to Jack and the rabbit hutch. Grandad and Jack had just finished nailing chicken wire on to one side of the hutch.

"I'll help you with the hutch again tomorrow," she said. "There isn't much to do now, is there?"

"We still have to make the doors – one solid and one with wire mesh for each part of the hutch," said Grandad. He looked at Jack. "But I've got a great little helper here."

Jack flushed with pleasure. "Hoppy is going to love this hutch," he said. "I was in the pet shop in Walton yesterday. The owner showed me this special drinking bottle with a tube on the end. You fix it to the outside of the cage and then the water stays clean. I'm saving up for one."

Mandy examined the hutch. What a perfect home it was going to be for Jack's rabbit. She smiled to herself as Jack talked eagerly about Hoppy and his hutch. Jack had certainly changed since Hoppy had come into his life.

8

Hoppy's new home

"Breakfast!" Mrs Hope called.

Mandy raced downstairs and into the kitchen at Animal Ark. Mrs Hope turned from the cooker and put a dish of fluffy scrambled eggs on the table just as Mr Hope came through the door.

"That looks good," he said, helping himself.

Mrs Hope set down a rack of toast and the teapot and settled herself at the table. Mandy looked round the room. She loved the kitchen at Animal Ark with its old oak beams and the copper pans hanging down from them. The red check curtains at the open window fluttered in the summer breeze. Mandy sighed with contentment.

"You look happy," Mr Hope said with a smile.

Mandy nodded. "I'm going to Laura's with Jack today to pick up his rabbit."

Mrs Hope poured the tea and looked at Mandy. "How are you getting the rabbit back to Jack's house?" she asked.

"I thought I would borrow a small animal carrier from here," Mandy said. "If that's OK?"

Her father chewed thoughtfully on a piece of toast. "Make sure you line it with some of the bedding from Fluffy's hutch," he said. "Rabbits have a very good sense of smell. If the new hutch smells familiar the baby rabbit will settle more quickly."

"I will," said Mandy. "Thanks, Dad!"

She looked at her watch. "I'd better go. Jack will be waiting."

"Have a good time," said Mrs Hope.

Mandy's face was shining. "Oh, I will," she said. "Jack is so excited. Grandad was taking the hutch round to help him set it up first thing this morning. I hope everything went OK."

Jack was waiting for her at the front gate when she got to Laura's. She looked at the little boy's excited face. "Come on," Mandy said, opening the gate. "Let's go and get him."

"He's all ready," Laura said as she opened the door to them. "I told him you were coming for him today."

She led the way through the hall and out of the back door into garden. "There," she said.

Jack walked slowly towards the hutch. Fluffy looked up, her nose twitching.

"Hello, Fluffy," Mandy said, bending closer to the hutch and putting a finger through the mesh.

Fluffy wiggled her ears and sniffed at Mandy's outstretched finger. There were two baby rabbits in the hutch with her. They were both black and white like their mother. Mandy hadn't seen the baby rabbits since they had left the nesting-box but she knew Jack had been to see Hoppy nearly every day. Jack and Laura were great friends now.

"Where are all the rest of the babies?" Mandy said.

Laura sighed. "Mum said I could only keep one for myself," she said. "We found homes for all the others."

She opened the hutch door and picked one of the baby rabbits up very gently.

"Look," she said. "I chose this one. I'm going to call him Patch."

"Was it easy finding homes for all the rest?" asked Mandy.

Laura nodded. "Oh, yes," she said. "Once Jack started telling people about Hoppy, everybody wanted one."

Mandy looked at Jack. No wonder she hadn't seen so much of him at school

334

recently. He was obviously making friends – and that was even before he'd got Hoppy home.

Mandy opened the carrier box she had brought. She scooped some of the old bedding out of Fluffy's hutch and spread it in among the clean newspapers in the bottom of the carrier.

"Dad says the smell of Fluffy's bedding will help Hoppy to settle down better," she said.

Laura nodded and put Patch back into the hutch.

"There, Fluffy," she said. "You take care of Patch." She gave Fluffy a pat. "She's so thin and her coat looks really dull."

"That's only because she's used up all her energy feeding her babies," Mandy said. "She'll be back to normal soon."

"That's what Mum says," said Laura. "But I still feel sorry for her. Especially since she's had to say goodbye to all her babies – except Patch." She turned to Jack. "Do you want to take Hoppy out?"

Jack nodded and moved towards the

hutch. "How do I pick him up?" he said.

"Just like I did," said Laura. "He's small enough to sit in your hand. But when he grows bigger you'll have to pick him up by the scruff of the neck."

Jack looked alarmed.

"It's easy," said Laura. "And it doesn't hurt the rabbit. Look!" She reached into the hutch and picked Fluffy up, holding on to the fur at the back of the rabbit's neck with one hand and supporting her bottom with the other.

Jack reached into the hutch and gathered Hoppy gently into his hands. "This is easier," he said.

Mandy smiled. "Well done, Jack," she said as he carried Hoppy over to the carrier. "And if you let him lie along your arm with his head snuggled into the crook of your elbow, he'll let you carry him quite happily."

Jack laid the little rabbit along his arm. Hoppy looked up at him with big dark eyes. "He doesn't reach the crook of my elbow," he said, laughing.

"Not yet," Mandy said. "But rabbits grow fast."

Hoppy pushed against Jack's arm with his back legs. "Look at that," said Jack. "He's really strong already."

"That's why rabbits are so good at hopping," Laura said. "They have such strong back legs."

Mandy stroked Hoppy's black and white coat gently and the little animal settled down.

Laura turned to Mandy. "I can't wait for the picnic," she said. "I'm really looking forward to the rabbit race."

"The rabbit race," said Jack, looking thoughtful. "You'd like that, wouldn't you, Hoppy?"

Jack put the little rabbit gently into the carrier. Hoppy began snuffling round, twitching his nose and sniffing at the bedding.

"I can't wait to get him home," said Jack. "Do you think he'll like his new hutch?"

"After all the work you and Grandad

338

put into it?" Mandy said. "He'll love it! Just you wait and see."

"Oh, Jack, that's perfect!" Mandy said when she saw the hutch in Jack's garden.

The hutch stood about a metre off the ground on sturdy wooden legs, well out of reach of cats. It was placed in the angle of a south facing wall, just where the kitchen joined the main house.

"Do you think it'll be all right there?" Jack asked anxiously. "Your grandad thought that was the right place."

Mandy smiled at him. "Of course it will," she said. "No draughts and it'll get lots of sunshine." She laid her hand on the felt covered roof. It stuck out beyond the front of the hutch so that no rain could get in. Grandad had thought of everything. "And that's perfect too," she said. "Hoppy will be warm and dry in there."

The kitchen door opened and Mrs Gardiner looked out. She was wearing a pair of baggy paint-stained dungarees and her hair was tied up in a bright blue scarf.

"Oh, you're back," she said to Jack. "Hello, Mandy." Then she caught sight of Hoppy. "Oh, isn't he gorgeous!" she said.

"Beautiful," Mandy said looking at Hoppy. The little rabbit was sitting back on his haunches washing his ears.

There was a call from inside the house and Mrs Gardiner looked round.

"Just coming," she called back. She looked at Mandy. "I don't think this house will ever be ready," she said. "And I've got the first guests booked in for the end of the month." She drew a hand over her forehead. "Can you fix yourselves some drinks? There's orange juice in the fridge."

Mandy nodded. "Once we've got Hoppy bedded down," she said.

Jack smiled. "Animals first," he said.

"If you need some food for Hoppy, help yourselves out of the vegetable basket," Mrs Gardiner said as she disappeared back into the house.

Mandy and Jack looked at each other.

"What now?" said Jack.

"First the bedding," Mandy said. "Then food and water."

"Right," said Jack. "Come and see what I've got."

Jack had collected a whole pile of old newspapers.

"Mum and I divided them up," he said. "She needed lots to cover the floor while they're decorating."

"These are great," said Mandy. "We should put four or five layers of newspaper in the bottom of the hutch."

"And I've got lots of sawdust and wood shavings," said Jack, opening a black plastic bin-bag. He grinned. "Dad's been doing a lot of sawing and I got some from your grandad too."

Mandy finished laying the newspapers in the hutch and scooped up a few handfuls of shavings and sawdust. She covered the newspapers with the mixture and smoothed it out.

"That should do," she said, looking at it. "Now, what else do we need?"

"Straw," said Jack. "For Hoppy's bedroom."

Jack opened another bin-bag and pulled out some straw. It smelled sweet and fresh. He unlatched the wooden door of the sleeping compartment and spread the straw out on the floor. "There," he said. "Now all we need is food and water and we can put Hoppy in."

Jack disappeared into the kitchen and

came out carrying a box of rabbit cereal mix and a heavy earthenware dog-bowl.

"This was Fred's bowl," he said. His bottom lip trembled a little.

Mandy looked at the bowl. "It's lovely," she said gently. "And I'm sure Fred would be glad that it's Hoppy's now.'

Jack nodded. "He would, wouldn't he?" he said. Mandy saw him blink some tears away. Then he placed the bowl firmly inside the hutch. "It's yours now, Hoppy," he said. Then he started opening the cereal packet. "You're going to like this."

Mandy gave a little sigh of relief. Jack would never forget Fred but it looked as if he would get over his sadness with Hoppy to care for.

"What about water?" she asked as Jack poured cereal into the bowl.

"I bought one of those plastic bottles," said Jack.

Mandy nodded. "They're good," she said. "The water doesn't get dirty or spilled."

Soon they had the hutch ready. Mandy washed some vegetables and chopped them up very small, mixing them in with the cereal.

"You can give him wild plants as well," said Mandy. "So long as you don't pick them from the side of a busy road."

"Why not?" said Jack.

"Because they would be dirty and covered with car exhaust fumes," said Mandy.

"What kind of wild plants?" Jack asked.

"Oh, dandelions and dock leaves and clover," said Mandy. "But not too much clover. And definitely not buttercups. They'd make him ill. I can show you some if you like."

Jack shook his head. "There's such a lot to learn," he said.

Mandy nodded. "I know," she said. "But you'll soon get used to looking after him."

Jack fitted the water bottle on to the wire mesh of the hutch and they stood back and looked at it.

"Have we forgotten anything?" he asked.

Mandy shook her head. "I don't think so," she said. She frowned. "He'll need a piece of wood or a branch to gnaw on so that his teeth don't get too long. But that can wait."

"So, can we put him in his new home now?" said Jack, bursting with impatience.

Mandy smiled at him. "*You* can," she said. "He's your pet."

Jack bent down and carefully took Hoppy out of the carrier. He stood for a moment stroking his ears before he opened the door of the hutch and placed the little creature gently inside.

"My pet," he said. "And I'm going to take such good care of him."

9

The race

Mandy hardly saw James for the next week. Every spare moment he could get he spent practising for the go-kart race. One day he called round to Animal Ark — to see if she would time him.

"Time you?" Mandy said.

James nodded. "Down Beacon Hill," he said. "I borrowed a stopwatch from Dad."

So Mandy spent the next few days timing James as he raced down Beacon Hill in *Cheetah*. He wasn't the only one. Andrew was there, and Peter and a few other boys including Gary Roberts. Pam and Jill had decided to enter as well. Pam's mum was doing a night class in joinery and had helped Pam with her go-kart. It was painted in tiger stripes and looked good. Gary's was painted to look like a snake. But Jill's looked a bit odd. It was painted to look like a car.

"It was my cousin's," she explained. "I just got it yesterday. I haven't had time to paint it yet."

"You don't have to," said Gary. "Just pretend it's a jaguar."

"Oh, great idea," laughed Jill. "Like a Jaguar car. I think your snake looks really good, Gary."

"It's an anaconda," Gary said proudly.

The air was filled with shouts as they all raced one another again and again.

"Just watch out for the river," Mandy yelled as James raced past her for a third time. "I don't want to have to fish you out."

By the time the day of the picnic came they were all in top form. But Mandy thought James and Andrew were the best drivers.

"Of course you've practised enough," Mandy said to James as they stood at the start line on Beacon Hill. "Grandad says you're a great driver."

James looked down at *Cheetah*.

"It really is a terrific go-kart," he said.

There was a huge banner saying Animal Antics stretched across the starting line. It had pictures of animals crawling and jumping and running in and out of all the letters. The sun was shining and Welford Village School was having the best picnic ever.

Beacon Hill sloped all the way down to the bridge over the river. Andrew, Peter and James had marked out the course for the go-kart race with coloured flags on poles.

"It looks really professional," Mandy said to Sarah Drummond beside her.

Sarah nodded. "Just so long as nobody goes into the river," she said.

"Mrs Garvie made sure the course went in the other direction at the bottom," James said.

The girls looked. The course followed the slope of the hill down to the bottom then turned off in a wide sweep well away from the river.

"Look!" said Sarah. "The go-karts are starting to line up."

"Better get going, James," said Amy Fenton, walking up to them.

"Wish me luck then," James said to Mandy.

Mandy grinned. "Good luck!" she said.

Then Mrs Garvie asked the racers to line up at the start line beside their go-karts. Mandy watched as everyone stood beside their go-karts, ready to jump into them and take off as soon as Mrs Garvie blew the whistle. The seconds stretched out. Then the whistle blew – and they were off!

Mandy stood at the start line with Sarah and Amy, eyes glued to the go-karts racing down the hill.

Andrew, James and Peter were out in front but Pam's go-kart had gathered speed and was catching up. Jill had a bit of trouble as she and Gary veered towards each other. For a moment it looked as if they would collide. Then Jill straightened up and shot down the hill after the leaders. James was neck and neck with Andrew now. It was hard to tell which of them was ahead.

"Come on, James! Come on!" Mandy yelled, jumping up and down.

All around her people were yelling their heads off as the go-karts raced down the grassy slope. First one, then another edged in front. Pam's *Tiger* picked up speed, threatening to overtake *Kingfisher*. Andrew's blue go-kart looked very impressive with its chrome wheels flashing in the sunlight. Then *Cheetah* came up from behind *Kingfisher*.

"Look, James has just edged in front!" said Sarah.

Mandy shaded her eyes from the sun to see better.

"Come *on*, James," she yelled again.

Cheetah sped on, its wheels sparkling in the sun, covering the ground faster than before. James was going to win! He was leaving Andrew behind!

Then Peter's *Terrier* put on a sudden burst of speed and flashed past both *Cheetah* and *Kingfisher*.

"*Terrier's* in the lead," Amy shouted. "Go for it, Peter!"

But then disaster struck. Peter's go-kart went over a bump and spun round right in front of *Cheetah*. James swerved, just missing him. But he had lost ground and they were almost at the finishing line. *Kingfisher* swooped past and crossed the line in first place.

The other go-karts were catching up, as they swept down the hill behind James but he managed to stay in front. He came in second, right on Andrew's heels.

The watchers cheered from the hilltop.

"Bad luck, James," Mandy said.

"If *Terrier* hadn't crashed, *Cheetah* might have won," said Amy.

"Do you think Peter is OK?" asked Mandy.

Jill nodded as Peter picked himself up and waved to the crowd. "Looks like it," she said.

Mandy watched them all trudge back up the hill pulling their go-karts. They seemed to have enjoyed the race.

"You did great, James," said Mandy as James came up. "I think you did really well to come second."

"So do I," said James. "I can't wait to tell your grandad!"

"I won! I won!" Laura Baker shouted, running over the grass towards Mandy.

Mandy looked down at the little girl.

"I won the hedgehog race," said Laura. "I can roll better than anybody else."

Mandy looked at the grass stains on Laura's shorts. "I can see that, Laura," she said, laughing.

Sarah Drummond pushed a trolley full of packed lunches and cartons of juice over to them.

"Mrs Garvie says we can have one more race before the picnic," she said to Mandy. "What should it be?"

Mandy looked at the clipboard she was holding.

"The rabbit race," she said.

"The rabbit race!" Laura yelled. "Wow! I bet I'll win."

And she raced off to the start line. Mandy watched her go. Laura was full of energy.

"I've brought Hoppy," said a voice beside her.

Mandy looked round. Jack was standing there with Hoppy's carrier box in his arms. He opened the lid for Mandy to see.

"Oh, he's lovely," said Mandy, tickling Hoppy under the chin. "And look how much he's grown!"

The little rabbit twitched his ears and rubbed his nose with his tiny paws.

"He can run really fast now," said Jack. "I'm sure he'll win."

Mandy was puzzled. "Win what, Jack?" she said.

"The rabbit race," Jack said.

Mandy blinked. "But it isn't a *real* rabbit race," she said. "It's like all the other races. You have to pretend you're an animal and race that way."

"You mean it isn't a race for rabbits?" Jack said.

Mandy shook her head. "It's for people, Jack," she said. "Look!"

Mandy and Jack watched as Mrs Garvie blew a whistle for the race to start. It was a sack race. The line of competitors hopped across the start, holding on to their sacks.

Some of them wore silly paper rabbit ears. "Oh," said Jack. "I wondered why I couldn't see any other rabbits."

Mandy bit her lip. He looked so disappointed.

"I'm sure if we did have a real rabbit race Hoppy would win," she said.

There was a yell from the finishing line and Mandy saw Amy Fenton throw herself across the line just in front of Laura. When she looked back, Jack had gone.

"Picnic time!" Mrs Garvie called. Soon there was a stampede towards Sarah and the trolley full of goodies.

Mrs Black, James's teacher, and Mrs Todd, Mandy's teacher, started handing out packets of sandwiches and cartons of juice.

By the time Mandy had got something to eat and sorted out the running order of the rest of the races, she had forgotten all about Jack.

She was lining juniors up for the snake race after lunch when the little boy appeared beside her.

"Can I be in the race?" he asked.

"Sure," said Mandy. She looked at Hoppy. "Just make sure Hoppy is safe in his carrier box first."

Jack ran off and Mandy turned back to the juniors again. "You've got to wriggle," she told them. "No running and no crawling."

The juniors looked up at her seriously.

"How about rolling?" Laura said.

"No rolling," Mandy said firmly.

Mrs Garvie put her whistle to her lips. "Ready?" she said to Mandy.

Jack arrived at a run and slid down among the other competitors on the grass.

"Ready!" said Mandy, and Mrs Garvie blew her whistle.

The juniors started wriggling.

"Look at that!" said Gary Roberts. "Maybe I should have brought Gertie along after all to show them how it's done."

Mandy, James, Sarah and Andrew stood on the start line, laughing. The juniors were all over the place, squirming and wriggling their way along the ground.

"Look at little Susan Davis," said James. "She's gone right off the course."

Mandy looked. Susan had wriggled her way right to the edge of the hill where the go-karts were parked.

"Hoi! Susan!" shouted Andrew. "Mind the karts!"

Susan turned at the sound of his voice and rolled backwards into Andrew's go-kart. It rocked slightly and she put out a hand to it.

They all watched as the go-kart slowly started to move downhill.

"Oh, no," said Andrew. "I must have left the brake off!" He took off at a run after his go-kart.

There was a clamour of voices as people turned to look at *Kingfisher* rolling downhill, starting to go faster.

Then a terrified voice shouted over the others. "Hoppy!" Jack yelled.

Mandy whirled round as the little boy jumped to his feet and began to run after the go-kart.

"Jack! What is it?" she yelled, running after him.

Jack didn't stop. "I put Hoppy in that go-kart," he panted as he ran. "I thought he would be safe."

Mandy looked at the go-kart racing down the hill – heading straight for the river. "James!" she screamed. "We must catch that kart."

James was already racing towards her but she couldn't stop. If anything happened to *this* pet, Jack would never be brave enough to get another.

Jack was fighting back the tears. "He'll be killed, won't he?" he said as he stumbled across the grass. "If the go-kart goes into the river Hoppy will drown!"

10

Runaway rabbit!

James ran to his go-kart and dragged it to the edge of the slope.

"What are you doing?" yelled Mandy.

"I'm going to try and cut off Andrew's go-kart before it gets to the river," he shouted back.

"I'll get my bike," she called. But James was already heading downhill in his kart.

Mandy saw James race off. His go-kart sped over the grass like a real cheetah. Andrew was halfway down the hill, making for his go-kart. Mandy made a dash for her bike and set off down the path that wound its way round the hill.

Down and down she went, hair flying, legs pumping the pedals. Behind her others raced, all trying to catch up with the runaway go-kart. Mandy lost sight of James as the path took her behind the hill. Then she was back on the same side again.

James had passed Andrew and was gaining on the go-kart. But would he be in time? *Kingfisher* was getting nearer and nearer the river.

Once again the curve of the hill hid Mandy's view. The next time she came round James was swerving towards the runaway go-kart, cutting across its path in a desperate attempt to stop it. Mandy held her breath as she saw James's go-kart cut in front of Andrew's. There was a crash as the karts collided. Then James tumbled out of his seat and lay, perfectly still, on the grass. *Kingfisher* and *Cheetah* rolled on towards the river and came to a stop almost at the edge of the riverbank.

Mandy covered the rest of the distance between her and James at record speed.

"James!" she yelled. "Are you all right?"

James raised his head. "Don't stop! Get Hoppy!" he said.

Mandy raced on towards the overturned *Kingfisher*. Behind her, the others rushed up, shouting questions, bending over James.

Mandy leaped off her bike as she reached the entangled go-karts.

"Is my go-kart OK?" said Andrew, racing up.

"Your go-kart can be mended," Mandy said, searching through the jumbled karts. "What about Hoppy?"

She looked round as a small figure came running down the hill.

"Hoppy!" cried Jack. "Where's Hoppy?"

Mandy looked at *Kingfisher*. Had Hoppy fallen out? Had the go-kart crushed him?

Then she caught sight of the edge of

the carrier box, half wedged under a wheel. Holding her breath, she lifted the box up and opened the flap. There, shivering inside the box, was Hoppy. He was terribly frightened – but he was alive!

James arrived, limping slightly, as Jack peered into the carrier box, his eyes huge with fear.

"He's all right," Mandy said gently. "Just a bit scared."

"Hoppy!" cried Jack. He gathered the rabbit up carefully in his arms and looked at James.

"You saved him," he said. "He was heading for the river. You stopped Andrew's go-kart. You saved his life, James. Thank you!"

James blushed bright red. "Don't mention it," he said.

But Mrs Garvie had seen everything. She came bustling up to them.

"Are you hurt, James?" she said quickly. "You were limping."

James shook his head. "I just twisted my ankle," he said. "It's nothing."

"Nonsense," she said. "You're a hero, James."

James blushed even more.

"I bet that's the first time a cheetah beat a kingfisher to catch a rabbit," Peter Foster said and everybody laughed.

Mrs Garvie looked serious for a moment. "I don't want anything like that ever to happen again," she said. Then she smiled. "But since it *has* happened I think we'll award a special prize for the most exciting race of the day."

Mandy looked at Jack. He was

cuddling Hoppy close to his chest. The rest of the pupils gathered round. Jack's face glowed with happiness as he proudly showed off his pet.

Laura stood by his side. But Laura wasn't his only friend now. Jack was one of them now – one of the crowd. And so was Hoppy.

"A special prize would be great," Mandy said, looking at James. "A prize for the runaway rabbit race!"

1

A new arrival

"I'm *so* excited about Duchess's kittens," Mandy Hope said to James Hunter as they walked along Welford's main street to school.

James smiled. "You get excited about all the animals that come to Animal Ark," he said.

Mandy's parents were both vets in

Welford. Their surgery was at the back of Animal Ark, the stone cottage where Mandy and her parents lived.

"But it's *always* exciting," Mandy said. "I think it must be much more interesting looking after animals than people. I mean, people are all the same. Animals are all different."

"Like four-legged ones and two-legged ones," said James.

"And some with no legs at all," said Mandy. "Like Gertie, Gary's garter-snake."

Gary Roberts was in Mandy's class at Welford Primary School. He had a pet garter-snake. Mandy always took a great interest in the pets of her school-friends.

"Duchess was in for a check-up yesterday," she said. "Her kittens are due any time now."

Duchess was Richard Tanner's Persian cat and this was her very first litter. Richard was also in Mandy's class.

James hitched his schoolbag on to his shoulder. "You'd rather have animals than people any day, Mandy," he said.

Mandy grinned. She loved going home every day to find out what new animals had arrived at Animal Ark.

"Dad says that too," she said. "In fact, so does Mum!"

"So does *everybody*!" said James.

Mandy laughed. James was her best friend. He was in the class below her at school – and he liked animals almost as much as she did. "You can talk!" she said.

"So," said Mrs Todd at the end of afternoon school. "You've all got to think about what we're going to do at Easter. Let's have your ideas. You've usually got plenty." She looked at Mandy. "Oh, Mandy, Mrs Garvie wants to see you. You can go along now."

"Me?" said Mandy, surprised. Mrs Garvie was the Headteacher of Welford Primary School.

"Don't worry," said Mrs Todd. "There's something she wants you to help her with. You aren't in any trouble."

The Headteacher's door was open when Mandy arrived. Mrs Garvie turned to her and smiled. There was a little girl standing beside her. She had dark curly hair and looked about five years old.

"Come in, Mandy," Mrs Garvie said. She looked at the little girl. "This is Libby Masters," she went on. "She lives at Blackheath Farm up on the moor and she's had to start school late in the term. I'd like you to look after her for me."

Mandy looked at Libby and smiled. "Of course I will," she said to Mrs Garvie.

Mrs Garvie smiled at Libby. "I told you we could rely on Mandy," she said. "I'm sure she'll take good care of you." Then she turned to Mandy again. "Libby's mum is coming to collect her soon," she said. "Why don't you get to know each other in the meantime?"

Mandy nodded. "Let's go and find James," she said to Libby. "You'll like him. He's got a black Labrador called Blackie and a cat called Benji. Do you like animals?"

Libby nodded, but Mandy could see her bottom lip trembling as she followed Mandy out of the Headteacher's room.

"Do you have any pets?" she asked gently.

"You mean, like a dog or a cat?" said Libby. She shook her head.

"Never mind," said Mandy. "You live on a farm, so there must be lots of animals around. You don't need to have a pet of your own."

The bell for end of school rang as they came out into the playground.

"Do *you* have a pet?" Libby asked.

Mandy smiled and shook her head. "I'm like you," she said. "My mum and dad are vets so there are always lots of animals around, but I don't have a special pet of my own."

"Hi! Mandy!" called a voice.

Mandy looked up. "There's James," she said.

James ran up to them, his face flushed. "Have you heard about the fancy dress party?" he asked.

Mandy shook her head.

James grinned. "It was Laura Baker's idea," he said. "Mrs Black was talking about what we would do for Easter. We had a picnic last year, remember?"

"I like rolling eggs at Easter," Libby said.

Mandy gave Libby a quick look. She looked a lot more cheerful.

"This is Libby Masters, James," she said. "I told Mrs Garvie we'd look after her for a few days. She just started school today."

James grinned at Libby. "What was your last school like?" he said.

Libby bit her lip. "I didn't go to school," she said. "I couldn't start. I had a broken leg."

James looked sympathetic. "That was rotten luck," he said. "It isn't easy starting late, is it?"

Libby looked grateful. "Oh, no," she said. "It's really hard."

"Was your leg very sore?" Mandy asked.

Libby shook her head. "Only at first," she said. "But I couldn't run about."

"You must have been lonely," Mandy said.

Libby nodded and her eyes lit up for a moment. "I had Ronda," she said.

Mandy was just going to ask who Ronda was when Laura Baker came running up.

"Did James tell you about the Easter party?" she said to Mandy. "It's fancy dress. Jack Gardiner and I are going to go as Easter bunnies. We're going to make bunny masks with big front teeth and huge ears. What will you go as, Mandy?"

Mandy laughed. "I've only just heard about it!" she said.

"Isn't it great that Jack and I both have rabbits?" Laura said. "Mrs Black says we can bring them with us to the party."

James's face lit up. "Does that mean I can take Blackie?" he said.

"Blackie would love to come," said Mandy.

If you like *Animal Ark*® then you'll love *Animal Action!*
Subscribe for just **£8** and you can look forward to six
issues of *Animal Action* magazine, throughout the year.
Each issue of *Animal Action* is bursting with animal
news and features, competitions and fun and games! Plus,
when you subscribe, you'll become a free *Animal Action*
Club member too, so we'll send you a fab joining pack
and FREE donkey notepad and pen!

To subscribe, simply complete the form below – a photocopy is fine – and send it with a
cheque for £8 (made payable to RSPCA) to RSPCA Animal Action Club, Wilberforce Way,
Southwater, Horsham, West Sussex RH13 9RS.

Don't delay, join today!

Name:

Address:

Postcode: Date of birth:

Signature of parent/guardian:

Data Protection Act: This information will be held on   sed only by the RSPCA.
Please allow 28 days for delivery. **AACHOD07**